False Start

False Start

a novel by Marissa Alexa McCool

Based on an idea by
Marissa McCool
Alice King
Jamie Plancher
Josh Rad

Foreword by
Kathleen Van Cleve

Post-script essays by
Lucinda Lugeons
Tanya Simpson
Fred Sims
Christin Kapp
Matt Briner
Sarah Ekholm
Marissa Alexa McCool

Cover design by Terry Sheffield at Mind Aquarium
https://www.facebook.com/MindAquarium/

Published by Wyrmwood Publishing & Editing
http://www.wyrmwoodpublishing.com

ISBN-13: 9781544827551
ISBN-10: 1544827555

Acknowledgements

My family (blood and chosen): Orrville, Alice King, Josh Rad, Jamie Plancher, Kathy Van Cleve, Lucinda Lugeons, Noah Lugeons, Eli Bosnick, Anna Bosnick, Heath Enright, Andrew Torrez, Stephanie St. Amour, Callie Wright, Tom and Cecil, Emory Van Cleve, Kris Napier, Marion Kant, Meta Mazaj, Kelly Laroe, Terry Sheffield,. Andreina Lamas Matheus, Brian Beccia, Ari Stillman, Jeremiah Traeger, Fred Sims, Amber Biesecker, Amber Johnson, Brittany Ralston, Natalie Garcia, Ingrid Stone, Chelsi Waffle and her amazing son, Chris Kluwe, Carmen Crone, Donovan Gruebele, Dan Bugbee, Tasha Bender, Brenton Bender, Nevin Ensminger, Shane Charleson, Greg Johnson, Matt Briner, Erin Cross, Tom Hackett, Jessica Ramaker, Raija Langhoff, Ilan Wolf, Robert Ray, Molly Un-Mormon, Louis Mendez, Robert Daniels, Jill Ramaker, David Benbow, Amber Benbow, Ben Cleveland, Bret Stewart, Jerry Cleveland, Greg Reich, Brady Ramaker, Liz Poehler, Kevin Watson, Jason Valasek, Liz Valasek,

Heather Vincent, Chris Watson, Cory Johnston, everyone I met at GAMLive, everyone who has reached out to me in support or any other reason, and of course, Kayla Hunt Currivan, for adding me to JaNo, and every encouraging, awesome member of JaNo.

And if I didn't list your name, I mean no offense. I could write a whole book of those who have positively impacted my life. Or, you could become a Patron and secure your listing... Just sayin'.

*To Aiden, Michael, Kieran, Kate, Le'ah, Brittany,
Natalie, Eli, Anna, Aaron, Monk, Stephanie, Andrew,
and my Rissy Monster Army.*

*And to the Penn LGBT Center, too.
May those that follow me know of your kindness
long before I did.*

Foreword

Kathleen Van Cleve

"Go for human."

I know. It isn't very profound—it sounds glib, even. "Go for human," says the smug teacher, as if the students are aiming for something subhuman.

But that's never what I mean. What I mean is that I want the students in my creative writing classes to create characters who are human from the inside—characters who behave in the complex and sublime and awful ways humans do in real life.

In my experience, it is the simplest and hardest distinction for creative writers, especially because we often want to say something "important" with our prose in addition to telling a story. What happens often is that the "important" part gets in the way of the "human part" and bad "message" fiction is created.

What happens much more rarely is that the important part becomes enmeshed in the story itself, and readers are left knowing they have read something both real and significant.

Ris McCool has done this in her novel, *False Start*. It is both a traditional and modern story, one that is, above all else, about what it means to be truly seen by another person, whether parent, child, teammate, or friend. It is hard enough to do this in life; it is even harder to create such a narrative in prose, in a story that is accessible, contemporary and above all else, well-told.

I'd like to take credit for this; after all, Ris has been my student for a while now. Alas, that would not only be unfair but untrue. The fact is that Ris is no longer a student (except in the sense that we are all students, for our entire lives). No. Now Ris is a professional—and wonderful—writer.

As her former teacher, I am extraordinarily proud. As a human, I am moved. And as a reader, I am grateful.

I think you will be too.

Introduction

There are some people who will read this story and say something along the lines of, "Oh god, here's some gay guy who wants to live out his fantasy of being a woman."

I said something at the beginning of my last book *The PC Lie: How American Lives Decided I Don't Matter* that I'll repeat right now: fuck you. No, seriously—fuck you.

In the year 2017, we've just elected a president who likely doesn't see us as people, and a vice president who is a fan of electroshocking people until they either pretend to be straight or commit suicide, because after all, it's better to burn in Hell for suicide than for queerin', right, Mike Pence?

I struggled with coming out as transgender most of my life, and only in doing so did I realize how much I'd lied to myself and everyone else for so long. If you don't believe it was a sincere moment for me, go back and find pictures before my transition and compare the smiles. Hollow, vacant, and lifeless are the words that would describe them when you hold those smiles next to the ones I wear now. Don't tell me this is something I did on a fucking whim.

I started writing this story as a screenplay. Actually, this idea came from a project in Kathy Van Cleve's The Art and Business of Cinema class at the University of Pennsylvania, which is why I asked her to write the foreword. The idea started there, and I couldn't think of anyone better to ask for this particular book.

Along with Alice, Jamie, and Josh, we started to develop the idea of Logan and Ezra/Ellie while I pretended to not have an unspoken investment in this concept. The problem we had was the second act. We knew what we wanted, and we knew how we wanted to end it, but we couldn't figure out how to get there.

When our project didn't move forward, it was mostly forgotten, except by me. I managed to get to page 29, and there I remained stuck... for two years. Even in taking Advanced Screenwriting with Kathy, we did a read-through of what I had back then, and it was easily the most well-received piece of writing I'd ever had at that point. I was hoping it would give me some inspiration, but alas, I was still stuck.

"How do I get there?" I kept asking myself. "What do I need to do?"

Fast-forward a semester, and I'm telling Pastor Carl: "I'm transgender, fuck you!" in his face as he protests at my school by screaming at children. In nine days, I wrote *The PC Lie*, and by the end of those nine days, I was not only out to 95 percent of the people I knew, but the school was acknowledging me as I am, and as I always truly was. The silver lining to the mushroom cloud that is the Donald Trump presidency is that it motivated the fuck out of me in more ways than one.

I'd had the idea of novelizing *False Start*, as my heart has always truly been in prose as opposed to scripts. I spent four years learning about cinema to figure out that I really wanted nothing to do with the industry, and that's no disrespect to anyone who has gone further in it. It's not for me. I love books, and that's where I want to be.

However, a combination of all those things and a little group called JaNo changed everything. I've always written better when I've had a goal, and other people to support it. It's why I loved the hell out of online roleplaying; when I had a set timeline and topic to follow, I was able to do so much better. As of January 21st, I was over 80 percent toward my word count goal.

This is a story of a small town that I frequented as a child, and may never see again. My grandmother may never read this story, but even if she never accepts my identity, I couldn't set the story in any other place than Orrville. It was perfect for what I envisioned: a conservative little town that always seemed to have such a strong sense of community, but might be a bit resistant to someone like me if I was ever visibly queer.

Now, I'm visibly queer, and my grandmother doesn't know. She may never know. But most of the people in my life do, and you may be one of them reading this book. This is a project that has been near and dear to my heart for years. I haven't written a novel in probably four, five years, and I thought I never would again.

This story is not only my first novel in a long time, but it's the one that means more to me than all the others combined. It's the story I've always wanted to tell, but never quite knew how to until the right moment arrived. You're holding a piece of my heart that needed to be realized before it could be delivered to you, and I thank you for doing so.

Words cannot truly express what the outpouring of support and love has been like in these last few months. Whether it's been on my personal page, because of *God Awful Movies* or any of the other number of podcasts on which I've appeared, thank you. From the bottom of my heart, thank you, all of you.

And I'll leave you with this: I promise if you ever need me, I'll be there. If you want me on your podcast or to speak at an event, I'll be there. If you just need someone to talk to, I'll be there. If you need a friend, I'll be there. Add me on Facebook or email me at rismcwriting@gmail.com.

Because I wouldn't be here without you. And the best way I can think of to give back to the thousands of people who have supported me, especially as of late, is to be the person I needed and didn't have growing up when I was still closeted and confused.

I love you all.

—Marissa Alexa McCool
January 21st, 2017

Chapter 1

1995

The small town of Orrville, Ohio was particularly energized this fall. Though rumors of the beloved Cleveland Browns moving was in the back of every fan in northeast Ohio's mind, the Cleveland Indians were distracting them with their first pennant run in forty-one years. Chief Wahoo seemed to haunt every street, be it on a flag, sticker, or car window.

While American flags were readily visible, one stood out above all: The Ramsay's. Huge, flapping in the wind, placed on a hill as if it were a signal to others that the fort had been taken, the Ramsays always had the biggest flag on the street. With Coach being a beacon of freedom for the military, as well as the high school's football coach, the most popular man in small-town America was never shy about his patriotism, his passion, nor the love for his only son, Logan.

At ten years old, Logan was already shooting up like a weed. Dominating for the local Orrville football midgets' team, he had "future Red Rider" written all over him, and it certainly didn't hurt that the imposing Robert Ramsay was the head coach. If Logan could grow up with half the presence and intimidation factor his father possessed, defensive linemen would have trouble both psychologically and physically bringing him down.

Stepping out from his house and heading to his blue sedan, identifiable by the US Army sticker proudly displayed across the back window, Robert unlocked the car with the click of his finger on the key. At only thirty-two, being the father of a ten-year-old boy was still a challenge, and the enemies that shot at him in simulated combat were nothing compared to the pressure he felt to be a good father.

Chiseled from stone though he might appear in his full, recently-pressed military standards, his heart fluttered with anxiety every time Logan took a hit on the field. His episodes were sporadic, but intense when they occurred, and since no trigger for them had yet been found, he couldn't be too careful.

After gripping the door handle for several patient seconds, Robert finally turned back toward the front door, which remained unopened to his dismay. Sighing, as he did most days around this time, he finally released the handle so he could cup his hands around his mouth.

"Logan, you're going to be late again!" Emphasis on the "again."

The front door opened, and Coach Ramsay's son dawdled out as if woken from a coma. His Orrville Midget

Football shirt clung tightly to his chest and he slung his backpack over only one shoulder like the cool kids did.

Walking toward his father, who knelt to connect with him on eye-level, he gulped. Even on his knees, Coach Ramsay was an imposing figure.

"You have the number to where I'll be, right?" he asked his half-conscious son.

Logan averted his eyes, either because he was annoyed at having to answer that question again, or because something interesting had happened to the left that made everybody happy. Robert gently gripped his son's chin back toward his steely gaze.

"Logan?" Robert repeated, the subtext indicating that this moment would not pass without an answer.

"Yes, sir," Logan conceded, his lips barely moving, lest he be accused of showing enthusiasm for anything that wasn't on a television screen.

"Good," Robert said. "If you feel an episode coming on, you go straight to the nurse's office and call me. We don't want another incident like last time."

"Dad…" Logan groaned again, having heard these instructions a few too many times.

"If that happens," Robert continued, "you don't go to practice, you head straight to Ezra's house. His parents know you might come, okay?"

"Yes, sir."

"Hey, Logan!" A new voice broke through the crisp morning air. Robert turned his head. Speak of the devil…

"Good morning, Ezra," he said to the young boy wearing a matching shirt to Logan's. Ezra strode around the side of the car, sliding free like a leather sole on a

3

polished wooden floor and formally returning the salutation.

"Good morning, Colonel Sir."

"Hi, Ezra," Logan meekly added.

Finally getting a glimpse of Logan's face, Ezra chucked. "Looks like you had a rough night. Should I start the coffee pot?"

Laughing, Coach Ramsay shook his head. "I don't think that'll be necessary."

Robert turned toward his son and kissed him on the forehead. His son resisted the affection to the surprise of no one who has ever met a ten-year-old boy. "Dad, not in front of the guys!" he protested.

"It's not the guys," Robert retorted, "it's just Ezra. Relax."

Robert shook his head once more, rising to his full height, which seemed to pierce the clouds from the boys' perspective. Ezra stood next to his best friend, as if to be his second in-command if anyone but Coach Ramsay gave an order.

Getting into the car, Robert revved the engine and backed out from the driveway. Coming to a stop before he shifted into first gear, he rolled the window down and looked back at his beloved son.

"Play hard tonight, Logan!"

Logan casually saluted his father as the engine roar faded into the distance. In such a quiet neighborhood, a loud one like that could be heard for blocks. Kenwood Drive was by no means isolated, but enough people lived there to be familiar with the roaring of Robert's engine. Given his status and respect around the town, they paid it no mind.

Walking down the sidewalk with his best friend, Ezra's eyes wouldn't leave the side of Logan's head. In the way that everyone does when they know someone is staring at them, Logan did his best to ignore it, knowing full well what Ezra was going to ask. Like many other times, it didn't stop him. Ezra was many things— flamboyant, enthusiastic, and intelligent among them—but the one thing he was not was passive.

"It happened again, didn't it?" he finally asked.

"Ezra, don't," Logan fruitlessly warned.

"It's okay, Logan," Ezra soothed, "I'm your best friend. I'm not going to tell anyone."

Logan's face reflected his conflicted emotions. On one hand, Ezra had never betrayed his trust in all the years of living in the small town of Orrville. But on the other, what better reason would there be than to gain popularity at the expense of the Coach's son? Logan could never be too sure.

"I just don't want to think about it, okay? I want to play football."

Ezra placed a comforting hand on Logan's shoulder. "I know, and you'll be great," he assured him. "But let's not pretend it's not there, okay?"

Logan smiled in response, something he wasn't frequently doing at that point. "I won't. But I'll try not to end up crying on your doorstep tonight," he joked, though the undertone was depressingly serious.

Ezra, smile as bright as ever, didn't miss a beat. "It's no big deal. My parents will make sure you can come inside. They know you don't always like being alone when your dad's gone."

A piercing car horn interrupted their tender moment. A 1984 Buick Regal sputtered toward the corner and let off smoke like the fire inside was from more than the hormones. Bernie and Jimmy, two of their teammates, stuck their little heads out the gigantic windows. The Regal's seats barely even held up anymore, and their leaning wasn't helping the upholstery.

"Logan!" Bernie shouted at the sight of Logan.

"Come ride with us!" Jimmy encouraged.

Logan blushed a bit, highly uncomfortable with the proposition of choosing between friends. Intuitive as always, Ezra didn't let the moment get to him at all. He nudged Logan gently for encouragement, but soon realized Logan was distracted by a pretty young girl named Erin Moyer standing on the other side of the behemoth death trap.

"Hey, Logan," she greeted him.

Logan blushed harder and looked down at the ground. Protecting his friend from embarrassment, Ezra picked him right back up. "Don't worry, my lady," he gallantly called, "Logan will be right along."

Logan turned away from the car and huddled in close with Ezra so that nobody else could hear them speaking. "Are you kidding? She's the most popular girl in school!"

"So the most popular girl in school offers you a ride, you take it," Ezra smoothly replied, motioning toward the car with his head.

Logan returned the enthusiastic hint with a glance of concern. "What about you?"

"Don't worry about me," Ezra laughed. "These boots were made for walking, anyway."

Logan blinked, unfamiliar with the reference. "What?"

Ezra chuckled and rolled his eyes. "I don't have time to explain Nancy Sinatra to you, Logan. Just go, I'll be fine."

Before Logan could resist, Ezra broke the huddle and spun him toward the car again, where the boys had been impatiently and obliviously waiting. "See, here he comes!" Ezra announced as he shoved his friend forward.

Logan glanced back, unsure of himself. Ezra took a step toward him and leaned in. "Go, she likes you," he whispered.

Logan finally got the hint and sprinted toward the car. Crowding in the backseat with his buds, he turned back to give Ezra a final supportive wave before the Regal mustered enough energy to move again. Ezra, looking on, didn't lose his smile as he watched the old car that would've been too broken down for Kyle Reese leave him alone on the sidewalk.

Ezra resumed walking to school, obsessively making sure his feet fit within the black mortar of the concrete streets. Secrets weren't meant to be told at times like that anyway, and Logan had enough on his plate, he reasoned with himself. There would be plenty of opportunities to tell his best friend the truth when the time was right.

Chapter 2

2002

The events of September 11th, 2001 transformed the nation. Where once only the Ramsay's flag stood, one now flapped in the wind on every patio, porch, and mailbox. The cars in every driveway had yellow ribbons and the words "Never Forget" plastered on their bumpers. Small-town America had redefined what it was to be a patriot, and Orrville, Ohio was no exception.

Logan, now an eighteen-year-old senior, donned a Red Riders letter jacket as he left his house. The old blue sedan that Robert had driven back in 1995 now belonged to him, and still proudly displayed a US Army sticker, along with its own yellow ribbon. As he drove to school that morning, many of the other drivers that passed him honked and gave him a thumb-ups out their windows. This was not an uncommon occurrence during Logan's commute to school in the past year.

As he locked his car and approached the red-brick Orrville High, he was joined by contemporaries in similar jackets and of similar mindsets. Everything around him seemed to stop for a few seconds as he noticed the giant flag from the football stadium dancing in the wind. Logan stood directly in its shadow, taking in the moment, and thinking of the many men and women in uniform.

The Orrville High hallways were covered in streamers, red and white crepe everywhere like a Halloween prank. Coming in second only to their country, the Orrville students loved their Red Riders football team, and Logan would stand next to his father, Coach Ramsay, as the star senior player. Undoubtedly, scouts from Ohio State would be purchasing Red Rider tickets this season to get a glimpse of the tailback.

He spotted Erin near his locker. It was hard to miss the head Red Riders cheerleader, even in the midst of all the similar colors. Her short-cropped black hair with a red strand stood out anywhere, and Logan loved her expressions of individuality. Seven years had gone by since the day he'd been encouraged to take a ride to school with her, and he'd never looked back.

It was good he got at least one thing out of that old friendship with… that friend.

Fellow cheerleaders Kathy, Jamie, and Alice palled around near her, exchanging stories about their latest ambitions and weekend plans. Logan approached cautiously, not wanting to interfere with any secret codes or handshakes that might be going on between them. He knew better than to disrupt the gossip mill.

Finally, when he felt safe getting closer, he slid an arm around Erin's waist and kissed her forehead ever so gently.

"You're late," she teased.

"What else is new?" he replied. This was hardly the first time he'd been tardy.

As they embraced, a companionate love grown over the years bloomed between them as if planted and cultivated only yesterday. Their cuteness really was the talk of the school, and how could it not be? What could inspire people more than the football star and the head cheerleader living up to Logan's father's reputation in Orrville, Ohio? No doubt they'd move on to become Buckeyes, living out their dreams on national television while the whole town watched. The new Ohio State coach was sure to recapture the glory the team had lost during the Cooper years, and what better way to kick off that era than with Logan Ramsay starting at tailback in the Horseshoe? O-H... I-O, indeed!

"Good to see you, Logan," Jamie said once his and Erin's embrace finally ebbed.

"Yeah, we were just talking about your dad," Alice added.

Logan paled. "My dad? Why?" he somberly inquired, the topic a sensitive note in the last year especially.

Kathy, surprised by the sudden shift of tone, chimed in to assuage Logan. "Don't get upset. It's no big deal."

"We just think it's so cool you get to start this year," contributed Alice, "and your dad's the coach!"

"What better chance at States could we have?" Jamie asked.

Logan blushed, and in an effort to distract himself from his glowing pink cheeks, his eyes drifted to the masses moving about the decorated corridors. Standing out like a maize-and-blue jersey in Columbus was a freshman named Josh, wearing thick glasses, a plaid shirt, and pleated khakis.

Poor soul, Logan thought. *He has no idea what he's in for in high school.* Logan's heart went out to him, hoping he wouldn't draw any more attention to himself.

But then two brick walls of flesh moved in front of him, immediately dashing his hopes.

Bernie and Jimmy stood above their prey. The two other senior starters, now splitting ends on the Red Riders' defensive line, were just dying to pounce on their newfound freshman treat. Logan grew anxious watching, feeling the urge to interfere, but he wanted to see where it went first.

"Looks like the frosh got lost," taunted Bernie.

Josh nervously cleared his throat and tried to move around the defensive ends like so many desperate opposing running backs would do this season. But Jimmy's beefy arm impeded his progress with little effort, forcing Josh back to the center of their killing grounds.

"I think he's denying our assistance, Bernie," Jimmy said with a smirk.

"It looks that way, Jimmy," Bernie replied in a menacing tone. "It's not nice to disrespect the seniors like that, is it?"

"Looks like the penalty's gotta be paid," Jimmy warned, looking at Josh like a slice of raw meat in the shark tank. "Them's be the rules."

Logan removed his arm from Erin's shoulders. It had gone far enough, and he wasn't about to see this poor kid get eaten alive by sharky defensive ends, teammates or not.

All the cheerleaders' eyes followed him as he stepped away. Kathy couldn't help but state the obvious. "Look like someone's about to go play hero."

Before the star tailback could give the freshman a hand, a red plaid skirt lampshading knee-high black boots and striped socks stepped right in his path.

"Hey Neanderthals," a deep, but feminine voice called out. Bernie and Jimmy turned around, and their faces turned white at the sight of the intervening party.

"What do you want?" Bernie demanded.

"Could you manage to not be a detriment to our species and leave the kid alone?" the girl sharply requested. This sarcastic plea for armistice confused poor Jimmy, who looked to Bernie for some kind of snappy comeback.

"The hell did she just say?" Jimmy asked, confused.

"I'm sorry," the girl responded, ironically unapologetic, "forgive me for not expressing myself in a series of grunts."

"Huh?" Jimmy still didn't get it. This wasn't a new state of being for the boy.

"Are you making fun of us?" Bernie retorted, demonstrating his brilliant powers of observation.

"You two are really quick-witted, aren't you?" The girl, quick with a joke or to light up your smoke, continued to spin their brains in circles. She gently grabbed the wrist of the would-be victim. "Freshman wing is down the hall and up the next floor, you can't miss it."

"Um, thanks," Josh nervously whispered, hoping this wasn't another trick. He scurried away before he could get confirmation on that, because the two boys were looking at the girl now, confused.

"We're seniors. It's our right," whined Bernie.

"We got the same thing when we were frosh," added Jimmy.

Walking away, disappointed at their lack of sacrifice, they noticed Logan observing. "Watch out for Psycho over there," Bernie warned.

Logan watched the two walk away, then saw the girl turn around to reveal her identity. Ezra, or Ellie as she was now called, was the intervening party. Their eyes met, but neither student said a word. Logan finally nodded in her direction, signaling his approval of his—he meant her, *her*—actions in saving that kid.

As Logan moved on, Ellie's eyes followed him down to the doorway, hoping at some point he could get past this. Today would not be that day.

Later that day, in the Orrville High locker room, Coach Ramsay stood above his kneeling team. Seven years hadn't done anything to change him physically, though a few wisps of gray under his coach hat were noticeable. His intimidating presence inspired awe from his students regardless.

Everyone kneeled around him like true believers expecting a sermon. Bernie and Logan wore numbers 79 and 99 respectively. Logan's number 32 honored his favorite player of all time, Jim Brown, whom he hoped to emulate one day. The team revered their coach just like the whole town did, but few outside this locker room were entitled to this kind of intimate encounter.

"Men, the season starts Friday," Coach Ramsay began, his voice resonating between the metal lockers and ceiling fans. "For you seniors, this is your last chance at a state championship. Your last chance to be the heroes you've all wanted to be since you were smashing into each other in midgets. You've grown up together, you've eaten together, you've bled together, and you've shared in the disappointment of losing to our arch-rival, Wooster, for three years now. Now you, and the underclassmen who join you..."

The sound of a metal door slamming shut interrupted the flow of his mojo. This confused everyone in the room. Nobody cut off the coach when he was rolling. All eyes turned toward Josh, nervously clawing at the steel door, as his backpack strap kept him from moving away.

"What the hell is froshy doing here?" demanded Jimmy.

"Yeah, where's your girlfriend, kid?" taunted Bernie.

Josh finally slipped through the Master Lock of the closed door, but the strap on his bag pulled him back and he crashed to the floor. The entire team burst into laughter, except for Logan, who dutifully jogged over to help the kid up.

"What are you doing?" he whispered, not wanting this poor soul to draw any more attention from the meatheads eyeing him up.

"Meet your new placekicker, gentlemen," Robert announced before Josh could reply.

Bernie and Jimmy shared expressions of further confusion. "Frosh is on the team?" Bernie asked.

"Bernard," Robert boomed from his sage on a stage position above him, "if you don't shut your idiot mouth,

I'm going to fill it with the toe of my boot, do you understand?"

"Yes, Coach," Bernie groaned, defeated.

Not content with that answer, Robert pulled the kid to his feet by the inside of his shoulder pad in an impressive display of strength. "Do you understand, Bernard?"

"Yes, General Sir, Yes!" Bernie pleaded, just wanting to escape the grip of the most intimidating man he'd ever seen. Robert dropped his shoulder pad like a bad habit, and Bernie crashed to the floor, stunned.

Robert turned to the rest of his team, watching from their one lowered knee. "If I get wind of any of you harassing a teammate, or..." Robert then pulled Jimmy up by the same shoulder pad above Bernie, "anyone else, James..."

"What?" Jimmy asked, oblivious.

"Anyone, absolutely anyone," Robert rumbled, "who is bullying, hazing, or just being an asshole will be kicked off this team, plain and simple. There are plenty of JV kids dying to take your spot. Is that understood?"

"Yes, General Sir!" the team responded in unison.

Robert's expression loosened a bit, indicating his harsh lesson had concluded. "All right, bring it in," he called to his boys.

The team swarmed around their mentor and leader, reaching an arm in as best they could. In a sea of pads and sweat, Robert still stood above most of them.

"We've got Wooster High in three days. They've beaten us in divisionals the last three years, and this time we can pay them back for it on our own field. On three: Go, Red Riders. One! Two! Three!"

"Go, Red Riders!" the entire team crowed.

Robert concluded the practice. "Dismissed!"

As they left for the day, several teammates playfully slapped Logan on the shoulder as he wandered through the hallway in a daze. The world was slowing down around him, and he crashed into a locker next to him. He sniffled a few times, but then wiped his eyes on his wristband and tried to get ahold of himself before anyone could see.

Finally stumbling outside toward the football stadium, he stutter-stepped his way to the first row of bleachers before sitting down, trying to regain his composure. Suddenly, a younger version of himself stood on the field, a replay of a memory from years past. Young Ellie, when she was still Ezra, was shaking his shoulders trying to get through to him.

"Breathe, Logan. Just breathe!"

"Let me go, Ezra," young Logan demanded, trying to pull away from his grip.

"You're having an episode," young Ezra pointed out, "and you've got to calm down before it gets any worse!"

"You don't know!" young Logan screamed at his then-best friend. "You don't know anything!"

Logan watched on, knowing how this story ended, but not wanting to relive it again. Young Logan shoved his best friend to the ground, then stared down for a second, realizing what he'd done, and offered a hand to help him back up. Ezra instead collected himself and got up on his own.

"Do you think any of those meatheads you call your friends will react the same way if you break down around them?" Ezra cried. "Do you think any of them give a damn like I do?"

Young Logan retreated to his place of emotional constipation. "Shut up, Ezra," he whispered.

"They don't care about you at all," Ezra continued, ignoring the warning. "Why do you care about what they think so freaking much, Logan?"

"Because they're the coolest kids in school," young Logan responded, "and you're..." He couldn't finish. He didn't want to say it, but he somehow knew he had to. Rumors had already been circling the two and their relationship. He didn't want to lose his friend, but he didn't need anyone implying that the two were more than just friends, so he knew he had to break it off somehow.

"What, Logan?" Ezra coolly answered. "Say it."

Present-day Logan's stomach dropped. It was like watching a movie instead of a memory that repeated itself in his head anytime he felt guilty.

"You're a fag, Ezra," young Logan finally snapped. "Everyone knows it."

Young Ezra's face went white and he turned away. Logan reached for Ezra's shoulder, but his best friend knocked his hand aside, destroyed by what young Logan had said.

"Save your pity, Logan," he said. "Have fun with your super-cool idiot friends and your new girlfriend. I hope they make you happy."

Young Ezra stormed off the field, as he did every time in this play. Present Logan watched his younger self cry out, "Ezra, come back!"

Ezra turned around at the edge of the field. "You said it yourself, right? I'm a fag. Can't have a fag holding you back, right?"

"I didn't mean it!" young Logan pleaded.

Tears veiled young Ezra's eyes as he stood there, betrayed. "You meant every word," he replied only audibly enough for young Logan to hear.

Then he left before Logan could chase him down.

Present Logan ran after him, trying uselessly to change what had happened years ago, but to no avail. He turned to see his younger self screaming into the ground. *Not again,* he thought. *Not this again. I need to get out of here.*

Logan sprinted for his blue sedan, desperate to get away from this haunting memory that had defined him for so long. He got home faster than any legal speed limit could allow, and kept it together just long enough to get inside the front door. He collapsed on the vestibule, similarly to how he had in the memory, and convulsed in hysterics. No longer able to control his actions, his limbs shot out as though he were having a seizure. His right foot kicked out a window near the door, and the glass sliced into his leg.

Robert, hearing the commotion, ran in from the garage and immediately dropped to the floor to grab his son under the shoulders.

"Logan, calm down, son," he instructed, having been through this many times before. "It's okay, it's okay."

"It's not okay!" screamed Logan. "It's never okay!"

"It's an episode," replied Robert, remaining calm as he knew he had to. "We'll get through it together."

"Leave me alone!" Logan cried, flailing helplessly, but the physically superior Robert kept him grounded. Logan finally let forth several more wails until he crumpled in his father's arms, tears streaming down his face.

"It's okay, Logan. I'm here," Robert assuaged.

"I ruined it. I ruined everything!"

"No, no, don't worry about that right now," Robert whispered, rubbing his back. "It's okay."

Robert held his son, who turned and cried into his shoulder, sunlight leaking in through the jagged shards still clinging to the window frame. He rocked him back and forth, keeping his distraught son contained with all the love he had for him. Nobody else could do this, Robert knew, and nobody else would. His wife had left long ago, and Ezra—*Ellie*, he meant, correcting himself inside his own head—wasn't around anymore. This was all Logan had.

"It's okay, Logan. It's okay."

Robert would cry himself to sleep later, on his own time, once he knew Logan could no longer hear him. He felt like a failure enough without having to let his son know he felt that way. It wasn't the time or place, and Robert had to be the strong one.

He knew it. He just knew it.

Chapter 3

World

The sun rose over the Orrville High School building. The noise of the daily commuters had yet to break the stillness of the morning. A sense of peace seemed to wash over the awakening wildlife, not yet disturbed by car engines and brakes screeching.

The small town bustled with life in the mornings, whether a trip to Buehler's was in store, the wooded park downtown, or even the Smucker's plant. The famous jelly family had, in essence, restored the Orrville from a fading light in rural America to a modern small town. Gentrification was in full swing, despite panic from the general populace over what was going to happen next, especially in regard to war.

Jamie and Alice were two of the first students to arrive at school that morning. The cheerleader friends had been nearly inseparable since birth.

"I don't think you're in touch with reality," Alice informed her friend.

"What are you talking about?" Jamie retorted. "This is, like, super obvious stuff here!"

"Oh, come on, you made it up!" Alice challenged.

"I did not!"

Alice came to a halt, turning to stare her beloved friend dead in the eye. "So you're telling me you actually believe that Shakespeare didn't exist at all, and was instead a made-up conspiracy because no one wanted to be a writer in Elizabethan times? How do you explain Marlowe?"

"I explain him the same way," Jamie coolly responded. "Except that one was the Puritan movement looking to bring down the heathens by hypnotic verse."

"And *Romeo and Juliet* was a vehicle of their diabolical influence?"

Jamie laughed. "Killing each other over a love that lasted all of three days? Teenage suicide?"

Catching the *Heathers* reference, Alice followed up appropriately. "Don't do it?"

"Nice," Jamie complimented.

The recognizable blue sedan pulled up in an otherwise empty parking lot. With dark circles under his eyes, Logan nearly shut the door on his own hand. He rushed toward the front door until ne noticed Jamie and Alice standing there, and he then did his best to shift into the persona he thought everyone wanted to see.

"Hey, Logan," Alice said.

Jamie didn't say anything, but she was confused over what anyone else was doing there at this hour. This was usually the time that Jamie and Alice could debate silly things without being interrupted by students, or even the faculty.

"What are you two doing here?" he inquired.

"Debating the Shakespeare authorship conspiracy," Jamie answered, frustrated that their discussion had been interrupted.

Logan squinted, then blinked repeatedly, trying really hard to open his eyes in the morning sunlight.

Jamie, oblivious to Logan's state of distraction, continued on. "You know, how people think a commoner never could've written such masterpieces?"

Logan, spotting something off in the distance, lost his ability to hide his state of being shaken up. "Yeah, yeah, Sir Franks and Bacon and all that, gotcha. Gotta go."

The pounding of cleats on pavement quickly guided the football star away from the two surprised girls. Logan darted toward the football stadium in the morning sunlight. Alice smacked Jamie on the shoulder.

"What was that for?" Jamie demanded, rubbing her sore spot.

"I told you this would cause deep-seated resentment among the peasants!" she cried, still trying to keep up the shtick between the two of them despite everything.

"Give it a rest, Alice."

Kathy and Erin approached from the other direction.

"Good morning," Kathy said.

"What's going on?" asked Erin.

Motioning toward Jamie, Alice snickered. "Old Grassy Knoll over here scared your boyfriend away."

"Grassy Knoll?" responded Kathy, missing the reference entirely.

"It's the Kennedy…" Jamie started to explain, but upon seeing the blank look on Kathy's face, gave up. "Never mind." She turned toward Erin. "Logan went to the football field."

Erin sprinted off toward the field, where Logan was no longer visible. Kathy stayed standing with Alice. "Weird morning," she remarked.

"You know who else had a weird morning?" Jamie asked, trying to return them to a more usual state.

"Anyone who took the Lusitania?" Alice quipped.

Robert Ramsay stood in the dewy grass along the fifty-yard line. The aluminum bleachers caught the sunlight, turning it into a funnel of reflection leading toward the school. Logan arrived, heaving a bit from his dead sprint, and froze before he could move closer. He wasn't used to seeing his dad this early, and couldn't help but notice that he was in full military dress, staring up at the giant American flag fluttering in the cool breeze.

"Dad!" he called out.

The old soldier turned toward the track, seeing his son jogging toward him once more. Logan dropped his backpack a few yards away and stood front-and-center next to his father.

"Good morning, Logan," Robert said.

Logan glanced around at the bleachers, before which he'd spent so much time pouring his efforts to help the Red Riders win. A sea of red started to envelop him, and football gear suddenly donned his person. A helmet in his hand, the cheers of "Go, Big Red!" flooded his consciousness.

He tried to find his dad, but instead saw the coach in his customary red polo and white visor.

"We've got time left for one more play. Go in and get it done, son!" Coach screamed.

"We've only got four seconds left," Logan answered, caught in the memory. "How are we gonna beat these guys?"

"I have faith in you, Logan," Coach assured his son. "I know you can do it. Go get 'em!"

Logan brought his helmet over his head, filled with all the confidence in the world, and ran toward his huddled teammates on the field.

"Logan!" Coach called from the sidelines.

"What, Dad?" Logan yelled back.

"Logan!"

"I'm right here, what do you want?"

"Logan!"

Robert shook his son's shoulders, snapping him back to reality. It was morning in the empty field, not Homecoming game last year coming down to the wire. Robert was there, in fatigues and not his iconic coaching uniform.

"I'm sorry, what?" Logan sputtered.

"What just happened?" Robert demanded. He'd never seen his son completely disappear from the moment like that.

"I..." Logan started, but looking around to see only the empty bleachers and the American flag, he couldn't explain what had just happened. "Nothing. What did you say?"

"Logan, I've been called back," Robert revealed. "The Army needs me to help in Afghanistan, but I don't want to leave you alone."

Logan froze in stunned silence. Robert leaned down, trying to assure his son he was still with him. "Logan, focus. I don't want to leave you here alone."

Logan, shaking it off, admiringly responded to the gaze of his imposing father standing in the shadow of the American flag. He couldn't help but be proud that his father wanted to defend the country so long after he should've had to.

"So you won't be our coach this year?" Logan asked.

"If I left, no," Robert replied. "Coach Bret Stewert would take over for the time being."

Robert sighed, not wanting to give up his coveted position for anything... anything but his country. He stepped toward the flag, seeing the wind gently blow it to straighten out the red stripes.

"Ever since your Mom left, it's been you and me, and we've done pretty well. But ever since those bastards crashed into those towers, I've wanted to do something. I don't know how much help I can really be anymore, but dammit! I have to find out!"

Logan looked on in awe of his father. He imagined full combat fatigues donning his father's huge figure, along with a giant military gun and dirt on his face. Logan couldn't help but smile at the thought.

"Dad, I think you should go."

This surprised Robert, who tilted his head to the side and chuckled a bit. "You do? But what about..."

"Dad, this is more important than us, more important than football," Logan assured.

"But your episodes," Robert reminded him. "What about those?"

Logan nervously shuffled back with his hands in his pockets. He stared at the ground, not having any reasonable answer for that. "I don't know, but... I don't want to be the one holding you back from getting payback for your brothers, Dad. Besides, I'm eighteen. It's about time I learned how to take care of myself."

Coach smiled, proud of his son, and put an arm around him. "Tell you what, I'll talk to Mr. and Mrs. Harris."

Logan's face went white, not expecting that. "Ez... er, Ellie's parents?"

"Sure," Robert replied. "They looked after you when I went on drill all those years, and they live right down the street."

"I guess you're right," Logan conceded.

Robert pulled his son in tightly for a hug, and then grabbed his face with both hands. "I'll be back before you know it, and our country will be safe again."

Logan hugged his father again, not wanting to let go, but feeling like he could never deny his father this honor. "Promise me you'll come home, Dad."

"Of course, I'll..."

"Promise me!" Logan's desperate plea split the morning air.

Robert took a deep breath, then gently patted his son's back. "I promise, son. I promise."

Erin reached the edge of the field, but stopped as she saw the moment shared by father and son. The sun slowly rose in her view, and the flag seemed to only cover the two Ramsays standing on the field. The hustle and bustle of students and faculty arriving drowned out the peaceful wind as what was just another day of school to anyone else was set to begin.

Chapter 4

Realizations

The world became the young man's oyster as the hallways parted for him. He couldn't tell, as everything was in slow-motion through his eyes, like a drifting glider. Erin approached him, saying something while hugging him tightly, but Logan couldn't quite make it out. Finally, shaking his head, he managed to get everything on the proper tracking again.

"What?"

"I said," Erin repeated, "I'm so proud of your dad, Logan! He's so brave."

Logan shuddered. Students he didn't know were nodding approval in his direction, almost desperate to make eye contact with the son of a hero. "Yeah, it's really great," he agreed distantly.

"Are you all right?" she asked him.

"It's fine," he said. "I'm just going to miss him."

Erin's face changed, expression morphing to what seemed like disappointment. "Now's not the time to worry about yourself, Logan," she chided. "He's sacrificing his time, the team… everything, for us. For our freedom."

"Of course," he mindlessly agreed.

"You should be proud."

"I am," he replied in earnest. He kissed Erin on the cheek. "I gotta go to class."

"Give your dad a hug for me if I don't see him," she requested.

"Will do."

Logan still had a bit of trouble shaking off the haze while walking away. Bernie and Jimmy approached him from either side to smack him on the shoulders. "Dude, Coach is awesome!" proclaimed Bernie.

"Hell yeah, bro!" agreed Jimmy. He's gonna kill himself some terrorists!"

The two high-fived behind Logan's head. The impact of hands sent a shiver down Logan's spine, and he kept walking away from his celebratory teammates. He passed through two heavy red doors, one decorated with a poster that said, "Beat Wooster!"

"What's up with him?" Jimmy asked.

"He's probably just getting that big game focus early, bro," Bernie guessed. "We're gonna destroy Wooster tomorrow!"

"All right!"

"Yeah!"

Later in the classroom, Logan sat quietly in the back row while everyone else participated in the discussion with the teacher, Mrs. Mazaj. A small American flag hung behind her head, giving her mostly-black professional dress an air of both color and patriotism.

"Many of those soldiers died right there on the beach at Normandy," she continued to explain, "but it was the beginning of the end for the Nazis. Just like our own Coach Ramsay heading to Afghanistan is the beginning of the end for the Taliban, right, everyone?"

The other students applauded and cheered, except for one, whose eyes were focused on Logan. Ellie, his old friend, watched on knowingly, searching for signs of concern. Logan shifted uncomfortably in his chair, trying to keep the overwhelming noise out.

"Now, while the soldiers stormed the beach," Mrs. Mazaj continued, "the 101st were dropping in behind them…"

Mrs. Mazaj's words faded into the background. Logan continued looking straight ahead, dazed, unaware of the several playful hands that grazed his shoulder. Ellie remained staring at him in concern while everyone else's attention returned to their teacher again. Logan wouldn't look up, but he knew he was being watched, and he knew Ellie understood what was really going on beneath the surface.

Just the way Ezra used to always know, he thought.

Later in the locker room, Bernie and Jimmy stood tall among their teammates while everyone took a knee around them. Josh, growing ever more comfortable in his new role, knelt right next to the defensive captains, and wasn't out of place. Logan continued staring off in the distance, barely aware a meeting was going on at all.

"All right, boys," Bernie bellowed. "Wooster is going down!"

"That's right," agreed Jimmy. "Let's win it for the Gipper!"

Bernie suddenly looked confused. "Who?"

"Coach Ramsay," Jimmy answered, surprised he had to.

Bernie still didn't seem to get it. "Then why'd you call him the Gipper?"

Josh meekly raised his hand. "Knute Rockne? All-American?" His voice sputtered with barely enough strength to be heard.

"Shut up, *Gimper!*" Bernie sneered.

"The nerd's right," Jimmy corrected, "and it's *Gipper*. You're riding in the back of the bus tonight."

"Aw, come on," Bernie protested. "Last time you put me back there, I got stuck sitting with the trombones."

"You'll have as much luck getting lucky with one of those as you would with the cheerleaders, anyway!" Jimmy taunted.

"Can it before I tell them all about the zipper incident!" Bernie threatened.

Josh stood up, looking toward Logan, who hadn't stopped gazing into the middle-distance.

"If the Bash Brothers are quite done," Josh drawled, "Logan, do you want to say something before we go on the field?"

Logan didn't hear a thing. Josh shook his shoulder. "Logan?"

Logan stirred finally, as if waking from a dream. "Huh? Oh… um… yeah. Let's go, Red!"

Everyone looked confused that their team captain lacked anything even remotely resembling enthusiasm. Bernie and Jimmy shrugged, then brought their hands to the middle of a huddle as everyone piled in.

"Win it for Coach Ramsay!" shouted Jimmy.

"The Gizzer!" Bernie proclaimed.

"Shut up before we send you to Junior Varsity!" warned Jimmy.

"Screw you guys."

"Go, Red Riders!" Josh called out.

"Go, Red Riders!" the team echoed as one.

In the tunnel, Josh, Bernie, and Jimmy parted the middle of the crowd so Logan could lead them onto the field. As if finally realizing where he was, Logan put on his helmet and ran in front of the giant Friday night crowd. Led by Logan, the Red Riders burst forth through the white banner that hid their presence from the fans, and the crowd cheered wildly. The Wooster team looked on from the opposing sidelines, ready for their rivalry game.

Near the bench, Logan stared off into the stands, searching for familiar eyes, when Jimmy turned him around. "Bro, you need to go on the field!"

"Why? We haven't kicked off yet!" Logan replied.

Turning around, Logan immediately got the answer. A full Marine guard lined up at the fifty-yard line, leaving one spot open. From the stands, Ellie stared at the back of Logan's jersey, looking for any signs of odd body language.

"Ladies and gentlemen," the PA announcer interrupted, "please rise and remove your caps for the men and women of the United States Marine Corps as they lead us in a Salute to America. Representing our own Coach Ramsay, our favorite son, Logan Ramsay!"

Logan trotted to the center of the field, but his mind drifted elsewhere again. Robert's voice shot through his thoughts: "I'm going to Afghanistan, son," and Logan felt more confused than ever, as the words he was hearing weren't what his father had said to him that morning.

The National Anthem began while Logan debated in his own mind what was real. Fireworks exploded during the "bombs bursting in air" part of the anthem, and the sound shook Logan harshly.

He stared across the field, and there he was! Robert Ramsay, in full fatigues... Dad... walking away from him into the darkness at the edges of the field.

"I'm never coming back, Logan," he called. "I'm never coming back."

The anthem finished, and the patriotic Ohioan football fans chanted "U-S-A!" in unison. But Logan was still staring off at the apparition of his father.

"Dad!" he thought he screamed after him. "Dad!"

Suddenly, the edge of the stadium exploded, spraying metal and flames everywhere. Machine guns assaulted Logan's ears, drowning out his screams as he watched his father disappear into the void.

But then Bernie and Jimmy jumped forth on either side of him, bringing him back to reality. Logan finally remembered where he was and dutifully jogged back to the sidelines. His gaze wandered off into the stands, and briefly he made eye contact with Ellie, who had the knowing expression she always did, seeing right through him. Logan quickly darted away, refusing to acknowledge that anything had gone wrong.

Later that night, on an empty, dark sidewalk in downtown Orrville, the stadium disappeared into the background. The lights in the distance overwhelmed the moment into indistinguishable whiteness.

Meekly pushing in the front door, Logan dropped his bags on the foyer and sat in his dad's recliner, his face completely stripped of emotion. The clock tolled twelve times to signal midnight, and each bell echoed through the house, reverberating off the wooden floors. A single light illuminated the entire bottom floor, barely peeking around the hallway.

The pictures on the wall held a vault of memories, eventually slimming from three people in the photographs to two. Logan's mother disappeared from the timeline as he reached the age of ten. The clock circled faster, turning into a circular whir like a ceiling fan, and the darkness of night enveloped Logan in silence.

Chapter 5

Falling

The Ramsay house was silent and still. The only sounds came from outside—birds chirping and the wind stirring the leaves.

Inside the house, Logan remained in the chair, watching a television that was never on. Images of a war zone began to flicker across the blank screen, bombs exploding in the background and men screaming commands highlighting the soundtrack. Amidst the chaos, Logan distinctly heard his father's voice.

"We're surrounded! We've got to get out of here!"

An explosion indistinguishable from the one at the football game the previous night made the television shatter into tiny pieces. Logan recoiled from the impact. Through the chaos, he heard a familiar voice calling his name.

"Logan? Logan!"

"Logan!" Jimmy yelled once more.

Logan rose to his feet, ready to fight whoever was in his way, but he saw the television still sitting there, perfectly fine and untouched. He looked around to see Bernie, Jimmy, and Josh surrounding him.

"How did you guys get in here?" he demanded.

"The front door was open, bud," Bernie responded. Logan turned to the front door and saw it hanging there in the wind, the morning light shining into the foyer where his bags still lay.

"When you didn't show up to the party, we took Josh instead," Jimmy explained.

"Dude broke down the kegger and had Kathy dangling all over him," Bernie added.

Logan tilted his head slightly to admire the nerdy young frosh, the very same one he'd had to watch Ellie rescue only days ago. Josh, however, was now the epitome of confidence.

"She enjoyed my collection of secondhand graphic novels," he bragged.

Bernie shoved him playfully. "This kid's crazy, man."

Jimmy, though, was noticing Logan's clothes unchanged from the previous night. He made the wrong assumption about the reason. "You hit a party too, dude?"

Logan weakly shook his head. "Didn't really feel like it," he admitted.

"After a win like that, why weren't you at least firing it up with Erin?" Jimmy asked.

Logan shrugged. "I guess... I'm just not handling my dad leaving so well, because..."

Bernie cut him off by holding a hand up. "Whoa bro, not cool," he warned Logan.

"Seriously, not cool," Jimmy agreed.

Logan blinked. "What?"

Even Josh appeared annoyed. "Your dad's on his way to fight for our freedom," he explained.

"You need to stop being a little bitch," Jimmy agreed.

"It's not like you're headed over there with him," Bernie piled on. "You need to get your priorities straight."

Logan finally walked over to the open door. Before he could close it, more teammates began coming through. Erin, Kathy, Alice, and Jamie also filtered into the passage. Erin kissed him on the cheek while her friends made nice with the other football players.

Tom, one of their seventeen-year-old teammates, cracked open a beer. "Party at coach's house!" he called.

The rest of the team jumped excitedly in response. A crash went up.

"Guys, don't touch that!" Logan chided.

Kathy, looking on and not impressed, wasn't having any of it. "Oh, lighten up, Captain Buzzkill. It's a party."

Defeated, Logan slumped as his friends started ransacking his house. Erin lightly tapped him to get his attention.

"Just have fun, Logan," she said. "Once you're dad's gone, we can hang out here all the time..." She provocatively rubbed his arm. "...and do whatever we want."

Logan looked away from Erin as the riot in his house turned into a blur. He sat back in his chair, staring off into space while Erin occasionally snuggled up to him. Her level of drunk increased dramatically in the midst of the chaos.

Josh and Kathy were arm-in-arm, leaving eventually with the plans of horny teenagers. Alice and Jamie ended up taking Erin away, all of it transpiring before Logan's vacant eyes.

Day descended into night, with Logan still sitting there in the dark. Snacks and broken glass lay all around him on the wooden floor. The house was silent, trashed, and Logan's shirt had been ripped at some point.

He stared back at the television, which was now actually broken. On the punctured screen, he saw Robert's face ever so briefly, shaking his head in disappointment and walking away before everything around Logan faded to black.

Chapter 6

Darkness

*K*nock-knock.

"Oh, Logan... hi," Ezra's mother said to the disheveled boy on her front porch. "Are you okay?"

"Yes," Logan lied. "I was just wondering if Ez—er... *Ellie* was home."

Mrs. Crow's gaze of concern flickered uncertainly at Logan's fumbling request. "Ellie? No, Logan, she's probably working on some project as she always does."

"Oh," Logan responded, still not sure what he was doing there.

"Come in for a second," Mrs. Crow instructed, to Logan's complete surprise.

"Oh, no, that's not necessary," he assured her, immediately backing away.

"Logan, get in here." She still had the stern call of a mother in charge. Logan silently agreed, walking through the door for what had to be the first time in several years.

In pictures adorning the family hallway, Ezra's transition to Ellie was marked in great detail. Football pads became mini-skirts; black paint beneath a young boy's eyes became eye shadow on a teenage girl's lids. It made Logan realize how little he had truly paid attention to his friend during their youth, because in retrospect, her femininity seemed obvious.

"In here, Logan!" Mrs. Crow called from a room down the hall. Logan quickly obliged, coming into their family room per her request.

He entered to find Mrs. Crow in a recliner, gently rocking a football with the Orrville mascot drawn on the side. Logan froze, unsure of what to make of this curious gesture. He hadn't seen Mrs. Crow in years either, and wasn't sure how to behave.

"Everything else in the laundry?" Mrs. Crow inquired.

Logan glanced down at his terrible appearance. In torn clothes that hadn't been changed in two days, he wasn't presentable to himself, let alone anyone else. "Guess I overslept..."

"On a Sunday?"

"Yeah, on a Sunday. Coach... I mean, Dad always makes me work out early on Sunday morning."

"Not the worst advice in the world," Mrs. Crow responded, clearly not talking about his physical state, but Logan hoped he'd wait out the questions he really didn't want to hear.

"Ellie always loved football," she said finally.

"Huh?"

"I know you think somehow because her gender is different from what you thought it was that her interests and personality also changed."

"Oh, no, I just…"

"Logan, let me finish."

"Yes, ma'am."

"It's not something a lot of people know about, being transgender," Mrs. Crow continued. "They probably don't talk about it in health class, and even if they did, most people around here faint at the thought of gay people existing, let alone someone who isn't their assigned birth gender."

Logan grew increasingly more uneasy, shifting his weight, not sure where this was all going.

"I didn't know how to handle it either, Logan," Mrs. Crow elaborated. "What are you supposed to say? What are you supposed to do when your child comes to you and says she's really a girl? That she's always been a girl? Why did she wait so long to tell me? Did she think I'd disown her, or worse? Did she think her father would throw her out?"

"That happens a lot," Logan said. "I mean, that's what I hear."

"She knows us better than that," Mrs. Crow said, not missing a beat. "We've always been an open family, to both Ellie and you, Logan. You know we've never told anyone your secret, either."

Logan blushed, realizing how vulnerable he was becoming. He tried to excuse himself. "I'd better go…"

"The point is," Mrs. Crow continued, "I know you're the big football star, son of the coach, probably the most popular guy in town, but I want you to remember who has always been there for you. Even before you were the big guy in the hallway. Even before you had the pretty girlfriend. Even before you had any other friends."

"I'm sorry, Mrs. Crow," Logan meekly stuttered.

"I'm not the one you need to apologize to," she informed him.

Logan scuffled along the concrete street. *Why can't we have asphalt streets like the rest of the country?* he wondered bitterly. The blocks of tar drew squares and rectangles along all the roads that weren't the old brick on Main Street in downtown, and it hadn't changed much since he was a kid. Orrville seemed stuck in a time warp.

The streets were all but deserted, likely due to most of the town sleeping off their rival victory party weekend. Not a single car made the red light in the square change, and Logan jaywalked carelessly through the intersection. He wasn't sure if he'd have stopped even if there was a reason to.

Every telephone pole in town had an American flag flapping in the gentle Sunday morning wind. *In case we forgot what country we live in,* Logan mused.

A mirage unfolded before him. He saw his father, but not the father that had left for Afghanistan. This was a much younger, sleeker man in his formal military dress, escorting a young woman down the walk.

Suddenly Logan was surrounded by an active, friendly crowd, pushing by him as he stared. The young lady reminded him of his mom, but... it couldn't be, right? Did he even remember what his mom looked like? It had been so long.

"You're a charmer, Robert Ramsay," the girl cooed. "What would your parents say about the way you're behavin' now?"

"I imagine they'd approve," Robert slyly replied. "They seem to like us military fellas."

Military fellas? Logan asked himself. What the hell was Dad saying? He'd never heard him use the word "fellas."

"Why'd you join the Army, anyway?" the girl asked. "You're gonna leave me all alone here in just a few days. What am I supposed to do with myself while you're at boot camp?"

Young Robert held the beautiful girl's hand in his own. "You could marry me," he proposed.

She flushed as she meekly reminded him, "Robert, we're only eighteen. We don't have a house, a job, or anything we'd need for that!"

"We've got each other," Robert said. "And I have a job now. Sure, you'll have to be alone sometimes, but I'll take care of you. I promise!"

"Robert..." she whispered.

Robert pushed her gently against the glass of the Mrs. J's breakfast diner. "Let's do it. Everyone says we're the best-looking couple in Orrville. Might as well make it official!"

It was incredible, watching Robert get all doe-eyed and pushing to get married at the same age Logan was now. Is this what led to the two of them being alone?

"Let's get married tonight," the girl suggested.

"Tonight? You want to elope?"

"You're leaving in three days, Robert. We don't have time to plan a big affair."

"And then we can maybe head down to Massillon afterward?" Robert offered, not subtle about what his intentions would be once they were there.

She gasped in mock offense. "You dog. I'm not that kind of girl!"

"You will be when I'm done with you!" Robert said, gently touching his hands to her lower back.

Nobody inside the diner bothered the love-struck couple, nor anyone passing by. The football captain and the prom queen tended to get a little extra privilege, so to speak.

The scene faded, and Logan's eyes welled up as he tried to repress his urges to scream and cry. He knew he didn't feel like that with his girlfriend. Hell, he didn't feel a close connection with anyone in this town but his dad, and Dad was gone. Dad and... Well, no, he'd ruined that years ago. Amazed that Mrs. Crow had even spoken to him, he recalled her tone in his head, surprised she hadn't threatened him bodily harm. He admitted to himself that he probably would've hurt someone who betrayed his child in such a way.

"I deserve this," he cried out loud. "I deserve all of this."

He sulked down the empty street, passing Mrs. J's where his parents had planned their naughty impromptu retreat. Several waitresses in the diner peered out the window after him, amazed to see the Wooster game hero in such a condition.

"He must've partied real hard," one of them laughed.

"An eighteen-year-old boy in that big house alone," the other one chuckled. "What'd you expect?"

Down about a mile from the park and the grocery store, Logan meandered to the cemetery on the hill near his house. He used to hang out there when he was younger, wandering through the trees and tombstones marking the graves of Orrville's past citizens. It was a nice place to stroll, and to hit golf balls on the vacant lawn between the headstones and the neighborhood. Signs indicated that no one should do that, but this was small-town Ohio, and he was a football star.

Logan pretended that he wasn't walking toward any specific area, but he knew he was. There was one in particular he always visited.

Gerald "Jack" Ramsay, eighty-one, died a few years ago, leaving Logan and his father officially alone. Now Logan's father was gone too, and Logan had no one except a resentful, but well-meaning former best friend's mother and her "telling him to do things but not really saying to do them" suggestive reasoning.

Alone, Logan thought as he knelt near his Grandfather's grave. Completely alone.

Logan removed the wristwatch he'd kept since he found it in his grandfather's room after he died, and placed it on top of the shining stone. He kissed the top of it before leaving it there, then stood up with little hope left in the world.

"I'm sorry I'm not as strong as you, Grandpa," he said softly. "Tell my mom I'll see her soon. If she's already there, I mean."

Walking away from the stone and tiny flag planted nearby it, Logan turned back for one last glance toward his grandfather. Apparitions of black dresses and suits formed around the stone, memories of the mourners who had gathered there the day Grandpa was laid to rest there. Grandpa had many friends, but only Logan and Robert left as family.

Logan saw his younger self trying to remain strong for his father, who saluted as the coffin was lowered into the ground. Young Logan turned away so as not to show his father his tears and stepped away from the group. He nearly collapsed against another stone, trying ever so hard to not lose himself around other people again.

Then Logan noticed something he didn't remember from that day. While Young Logan collapsed out of view from the funeral, someone in white watched on from the trees nearby. A white dress, flapping in the wind, covering two strong but nearly as pale legs, leading up to a familiar face.

"She was there," Logan whispered to himself observing the scene. "She was there. She was there for me, and I ruined everything."

Logan's urges were getting too strong, so he took off toward his house, the daylight shimmering off the many stones and several metal emblems decorating the cemetery. As Young Logan collapsed into himself between two grave markers that kept him hidden from view, one person had watched him instead of the ceremony from a safe distance. The one person who always knew what was going on during these episodes.

Chapter 7

Mirage

Drifting. Falling. Oblivion.

Into the late Sunday night before school, Logan watched his life unfold before his own eyes. One face kept coming up more than all the others, and it wasn't his girlfriend, or even his father.

It was her.

Or him, at one point. Should he remember her always as a her, or as a him when he looked like one? Or was that right to say that he looked like a boy? Why didn't anyone ever explain this to him? Ezra one day became Ellie, and that was it. As his best friend, shouldn't he have at least been given an explanation?

The pressure was too much at the time. Young boys can be the worst of people, especially Bernie and Jimmy. He didn't want to get on their bad sides, and he knew being seen with someone like *that* was going to get him bullied. Why did Ezra give up on being the popular football star's best friend? Why did he have to do this? Why didn't he take any of this into consideration?

"I mean *she!*" he yelled. "Fuck!"

He broke away from the stationary position and tried to run up toward his room, but standing there in the doorway were visions of Ellie's parents and his father, having a discussion about their children's recent interaction.

"Didn't you tell him…?"

"Her," Ellie's mother firmly corrected.

"Excuse me," Robert stepped back, embarrassed. "This will take a period of adjustment, but I'm trying."

"Ellie is a girl, has always been a girl, and will always be a girl," Ellie's father added. "End of story."

"Look," Robert snapped back, "I know my son can sometimes be a bit rough to deal with, but I'm sure he didn't mean anything by…"

"It doesn't matter if he meant it or not!" Ellie's mother screamed.

Robert sighed, then looked to see if he could see his son. Robert didn't lock eyes with him, but knew Logan was lurking nearby. He knew his son well.

"It shouldn't," Robert admitted. "I'm on your side, here."

"Right, like you military men are always on the cutting edge of social progress," Ellie's father snarled.

Robert straightened. "What the hell is *that* supposed to mean?" The coach was a generous, patient man, but having his commitment to his country called into question was not something he was ready to accept from anyone, even if they were close family friends.

"It means that he had to learn it from somewhere," Ellie's mother muttered.

"And it had to be me?" Robert huffed. "He's never been in a locker room before? He hasn't heard locker room talk that didn't come from my mouth?"

"Enough. I'm leaving." Ellie's father walked out. "Are you coming?"

"In a minute," Ellie's mother coolly replied.

Once the door to the car outside slammed shut, Ellie's mother grabbed Robert gently by the hands. "Robert, listen…"

"But…"

"No, right now I need you to listen to what I have to say."

Robert obliged, bracing himself on the bannister of the staircase.

"This has been difficult on all of us," Ellie's mother explained. "I'm not going to pretend that it's not a… shall we say, *unique* situation. But it's the hand we've been dealt. Ellie is a great kid, and she was perfectly within her rights to make this decision. We love Logan, and she does too, but he crossed the line today. He used a word that shouldn't be used toward anyone different, or at all, for that matter. It was inappropriate, offensive, and it destroyed the poor girl. She lost her best friend, Robert. Do you understand that?"

"Of course I do," Robert agreed. "But I don't see why they can't talk it out and make up!"

"Some things are too hurtful to take back," Ellie's mother answered as she opened the door. "And that's one of them."

Robert leaned against the doorframe as the Crows' car sped away from the slanted driveway. Even with that uncomfortable conversation, Robert hoped they didn't scrape the undercarriage. The incline was steep, after all.

He sighed, his forehead against his raised arm. "Logan, Logan..." he muttered to himself. "What are we going to do with you, son?"

Logan tried to reach out, somehow feeling closer than when he witnessed it from the top of the stairs. "I'm sorry, Father!"

A crash came from the back of the house. Robert immediately stood at attention, then darted up the steps to the source of the noise. "Not again, Logan..."

Logan watched his father move quickly toward his room. He knew what he'd find in there, of course. What he always did when noises like that were heard in the Ramsay household; one of Logan's episodes getting the best of him, and Father having to deal with it yet again.

"It's because of me," Logan whispered to himself. "Everything he's had to go through, everything Ellie's had to go through... it's all because of me."

"I didn't mean it!" he remembered screaming at Ellie on the football field that day. The look on his... damn, *her* face as tears welled up in her eyes came back to haunt him in the worst way.

"Yes, you did," she'd said, the memory of her voice ripping through his soul.

Logan felt it coming on, and there was no way to stop it. Nobody was around to save him this time. The house was a disaster, broken glass was everywhere, and the two people on which Logan could rely were nowhere to be found.

Suddenly, there Ellie was; as she was at the age when they last spoke to each other. Her plaid skirt flapping in the wind, the tear-stained face, her jaw when it was still strong before the transition had softened it... right in front of him.

"I could've killed myself because of you," she taunted him.

Logan couldn't comprehend Ellie saying something like that. Sure, she was snarky, but never that ruthless. She'd never taken any kind of action or vengeance back against him since that day, and Logan still wasn't sure why.

"I'm glad you didn't," he told her. "I'm really glad you didn't."

"No thanks to you," she sneered. This wasn't her. *It's not real,* he tried to convince himself. "Everything that happened to me, my parents, and your father..."

Logan's heart leapt to his throat. He covered his face with his hands. "What about my father?"

"Your father's going to die over there, and it's all your fault, Logan," she explained. "If he didn't have such a pain in the ass son to deal with, he probably would've stayed. But hey, if you had to deal with you back at home, wouldn't a warzone be more comforting than watching how pathetic you are when something emotional happens?"

"Stop," Logan, shaking and convulsing, pleaded.

"What's the matter, big football hero not able to handle a little girl?"

"Stop," he repeated.

"What are you gonna do without your father to protect you? Coach Ramsay being dead won't save your ass, will it?"

"It's not true," Logan tried to convince himself again. "He's not dead!"

"Oh, yes he is," Ellie snickered. "He was dead the minute you drove him away. He's never coming back."

"Stop…"

"He's never coming back!"

"Stop!"

"He's never coming back!"

"Stop! Stop! Stop!" Logan was screaming at the top of his lungs now. "Go away, and leave me alone!" Collapsing on the steps, he cried and thrashed, nobody there to stop him. Nobody there to comfort him. Nobody there to calm him down.

Except Ellie. The younger version of Ellie from the last time they spoke looked down on him with a crooked smile.

"Pathetic," she laughed as she disappeared through the door.

Logan couldn't find it within himself to disagree. The frantic crying took over the shaking, and in the shattered darkness, he howled for the one person he couldn't have back.

Once Logan regained control of his body, he disappeared into the cool fall night, heading toward the stadium. After all, that was the last place he felt somewhat comfortable, so it was worth a shot.

Chains kept anyone from entering through the gate, but Logan easily climbed over the wire fence. Being an athlete had its advantages. His feet slammed down on the track inside the gate, echoing throughout the empty bleachers that had been packed with screaming fans wearing red only two nights ago. Now it was a ghost town, holding only the memories of the triumphant and the virtuous. This was where he deserved to go out.

Slowly pressing down on the shiny playing surface, his feet carried his disheveled figure, the blood soaking in around his arms from the broken glass. He didn't feel it anymore at that point, with the numbness from the shock reflecting his inner spirit after two days of self-torture. *It'll all be over soon,* he convinced himself. *I need to make it stop.*

Without even the security lights on, the dark field enveloped him. No ghosts of past success ran by him. No former screaming fans tried to talk him out of ruining any lives. That had already been done by his own actions. He didn't deserve to be popular, or loved, or alive.

"This is how it has to be," he announced to no one in particular as he drew a particularly large shard of glass from his jeans pocket. "I can't make it stop." His eyes darted around for someone, anyone who might be there, but they again fell on only blackness and silence. *No one is coming this time,* he thought. *It's for the better.*

Logan slid his finger across the sharp end of the glass, and he cringed as it cut the tip. Blood trickled down his hand as he closed his eyes and prepared for everything to finally be put to rest. The source of all his misery, his father's worries, and the pain he put his friends in.

"I'm sorry," he told them, even though he knew they couldn't hear. "I'm sorry!"

He moved the glass toward his throat, but felt a shoulder spear right through his stomach. The glass flew out of his hand into the night, and his breath couldn't make its way back in. He heaved, rolling on his side and trying to suck in a breath. *Shit, that was a hard hit, whatever it was*, he thought.

Though it was nearly impossible to see, a silhouette stood over him, presumably the source of that gut-wrenching tackle. Nobody had hit him like that in years, not even the huge Wooster defensive linemen. Only one person had ever…

No, it couldn't be!

"What the fuck are you doing, Ramsay?"

Chapter 8

Confrontation

Logan's gut hurt like a javelin struck him, or like he'd eaten at Arby's the previous night. It was hard to make out in the night, but he knew who it was. Nobody on Orrville, or any other team, could hit Logan like that, lest they fear the coach's wrath. Only one person never lived in fear of pissing off the coach by hitting his son like a pro would.

"Hey!" The voice cut off his stream of consciousness. "Ramsay! I said, what the fuck are you doing?"

Before he knew it, two hands grabbed his shoulders, pulling him to his feet with relative ease. He knew the voice too, though it was different from how he remembered it.

A car drove by, and a flashlight was on them within seconds. Cops. "What are you doing out there?" one of the officers called out. A door shutting several seconds later indicated that they were coming to investigate.

"Run!" the figure instructed, but Logan ignored it.

"I got this," he replied.

Two of Orrville's finest jogged onto the field, both of them flashing their beams at the two standing near midfield. They stopped as they got closer, recognizing at least one of the people standing on the painted line.

"Oh, it's just you, Logan!" the officer who had called out noted, relieved.

"Ramsay, you dog, you!" the other officer congratulated him, possibly not being aware of who the other person was. "Your dad's been away a few days and you're already doing the Larry Kroger method of picking girls up, huh?"

"I…" Logan started to protest, but the person's hand covered his mouth before he could say anything.

"Make sure you're safe," the first officer warned him. "And try to be out of here before the sun comes up. Nobody needs a Monday morning explanation about this."

"We won't say anything if you don't," the other officer agreed.

Before Logan could chase them down and explain the situation, his partner in crime wrenched his arm just enough to keep him from following them. Once the doors finally slammed shut once more, the grip was released.

The police car gave a short siren blare as an acknowledgement, then disappeared into the night almost as quickly as it had arrived. Finally, Logan turned toward his co-culprit, desperate to know what had just transpired. Before he could say anything, however, the person started dragging him toward the school.

"What are you doing?" Logan protested. "The

school's closed!"

"Ramsay, shut up," the figure demanded. "I was working late on my project."

Project... Now he definitely knew who it was.

The heavy steel door creaking closed was accompanied by the bright, fluorescent lights sputtering on. Boots clacking across the granite floor echoed toward Logan as he was still trying to shake off the cobwebs. He wanted to raise his eyes to meet them, but he didn't dare, knowing what he had put this person through.

"You forget how to speak in the time's it's been, or what?" the person sneered. "What the fuck were you doing out there, Logan? For god's sake, answer me!"

Logan finally lifted his head, knowing who he was going to see, but somehow still shocked when his eyes met theirs. For a brief second, he and the girl he once knew as Ezra were ten years old again, donning midget football uniforms, and she was closer to him than any friend he'd ever had before or since. Lamenting his actions since that time deeply, Logan's head started to fall down again, but a strong, firm hand lifted it back up by the chin.

"Why are you so afraid to look at me, Logan?" Ellie asked

"I... I..."

"You're not a pirate. Speak already!"

"I didn't want to hurt you again," Logan finally sputtered.

"Hurt me?" Ellie laughed. "Pretty sure I would've knocked your ass out with that tackle."

"How did you..."

She cut him off. "My gender changed, Logan. I didn't."

She broke formation and retreated back toward the table where several papers were scattered. She started gathering them and neatly stacking them once again, trying to hide the presence of messiness. Logan watched on, admiring her ability to organize quickly while somehow still intimidating the hell out of him.

Being intimidated by a girl was sort of a new thing for Logan Ramsay. The only person who'd ever made him feel like that before was his own father, and there wasn't anyone, man or woman, willing to stand up to the legendary Coach Ramsay—not in this town, anyway.

As Ellie gathered a few more sheets of scrap paper, arranging them in several piles along a white prop-up table, she sighed.

"You football players get to be done with your work on Friday, and you don't have to come back to practice until Monday," she mused. "We get to spend all weekend writing about your gridiron glory in the school paper."

"You write for the paper now?" he asked.

"So you *can* speak in complete sentences," Ellie replied with noticeable snark. "Progress. And yes, I didn't just make up that anecdote for your amusement. Given that I'm sure you've never had time or need to check it out, it doesn't surprise me that you were completely unaware."

"I do!" Logan tried to disagree, but Ellie held up a hand.

"Logan, spare me. I've got a deadline to meet, and I don't have time for you trying to impress me by lying about reading the school paper. If you did, you would've known by now."

Logan conceded the point, and instead walked to the

other side of the table from where she stood, busily arranging different typed pages into a set designed to stand in for the front page. Completely aware of his presence looming, she kept gently moving the tips of some of the papers without looking up but not raising her eyes to meet him.

"Don't bother asking me anything else until you tell me what you were doing out on the field with a sharp object, Ramsay," she snapped.

Logan pulled up a steel chair and took a load off, in more ways than one. He noticed how efficient she was, arranging multiple pages and articles while also keeping an eye on his every movement. He didn't remember anything like this in their years of being so close. Matter of fact, he couldn't remember anything she liked to do back then. What do you know about your friends at ten years of age except common school activities and hanging out because you're the same age and grade?

Logan's mind wandered back to that time, when she was still Ezra. It was hard not to think of it as a simpler time, as cliché as that was, but everything seemed to be that way. Orrville High was the juggernaut of football in the area, and their midget football program was arranged by his father, who was of course the head football coach even back then. Coach Ramsay's universal respect in the area lent itself to many privileges, and getting to the division championship in his first year in 1993 didn't hurt, either.

So many nights they spent after football practice, walking home and talking about the other people they knew: the ones on the team, the girls who watched, the artsy-types who gave them no attention whatsoever. *What changed?* he wondered. *What took us from being best friends to having this tension hanging over us just from being in the same room?*

"I still pay attention, you know," Ellie said, interrupting his stream of consciousness.

"Huh?" Logan slipped out of his nostalgia and pretended he'd been present the whole time.

"You never could act for shit," she laughed. "I'm guessing right now, you were thinking about the good old times when there were no problems, when we were buds who played football together, and when you didn't have to think about what name and pronouns to use around me. Is that about right?"

Logan shrugged, desperate to not answer such an invasive question, but Ellie had always been the one who could see right through him. So after a moment's hesitation, he meekly nodded.

She nodded. "As I thought. Well, as I recall, when we got to junior high, you were too cool to be seen with me."

"It wasn't that," he interjected.

"Give me a break, Logan," she snapped. "All the jocky guys gave you shit for hanging out with a queer."

"That wasn't the word they used..." Logan needlessly, but correctly stated.

"I'm not going to use the one they did, because you did too," she snarled. "When did it become more important what a couple sacks of meat with eyes thought about you than I did? And exactly how many times did they help you through your episodes?"

Ellie was now demanding an answer for these questions, moving quickly from the rhetorical to the accusatory.

When she didn't get what she was looking for, she

stomped around the table and looked up at Logan. He loomed several inches higher than she did, even with her elevated boots, but that didn't stop her.

"Why was it so important to be liked by them?" she asked. "They don't know a thing about you except that you carry the ball a little better than they can, and you're the coach's son, so they have to kiss your ass! Do you think they care at all about who you are or what you still go through? Don't tell me you don't—I've seen you in school, especially since your father left!"

Logan couldn't argue. She read him like a book, just like she always did.

"You're right," he admitted, ashamed of his own actions. "I tried to apologize, but..."

"What?" she responded with fury. "You thought that one 'I'm sorry' could make up for betraying me for the sake of two dimwits who would bully me instead of you if you took their side? You thought that by being friendly with them, they would morph into the support system you needed?"

"I was afraid," Logan yelled.

"How the hell do you think I felt?" Ellie screamed back.

"I don't know," Logan sputtered. "I don't know how you felt."

"And that was the problem!" she exclaimed before returning to her side of the work table. She began arranging again while trying to get the redness to leave her face. "Yeah, we were great friends, and I loved you like a brother, Logan. But you didn't know a damn thing about me and never cared to find out. Then, once I was a little too queer for you to be seen around, you bailed the first chance you got." She slammed a plastic sheet down on top of the article she'd placed in the center of the front page.

"I would've done anything to protect you," she murmured. "I held you through so many of your panic attacks, told you it was going to be all right, and always had your back."

"I'm sorry, Ellie," Logan cried.

"Yeah, well, what can you do?" she retorted. "But if you thought I was going to stand by and let you do something stupid you could never take back, you're more dense than I ever thought possible."

Stomping toward the door, she flicked off all lights but one, leaving Logan standing in the dim center of the newspaper room.

"You know where I am," she advised. "I know your father's gone, and that it hurts like hell. Believe me, if anyone knows what it's like to lose someone they love, it's me."

Then she disappeared out the door, and those last words stung, years of bitterness and resentment mixing with the sorrow and regret Logan had internalized.

He was about to turn around and leave, but he couldn't help noticing the front page of the newspaper that would come out the next morning. It was a snapshot of him dodging two Wooster tacklers and well on his way to scoring his first touchdown of the night.

"Coach's Son Makes Deployed Dad Proud," it read in bold letters atop the photograph. Then, right under the title and beside the picture, "By Eleanor Crow."

"Orrville's favorite son eased the pain of losing their beloved coach to Afghanistan this past Friday by putting on a highlight-reel performance for the ages against rival

Wooster. The Red Riders defeated their arch-nemeses 38-21, with star running back Logan Ramsay leading the way..."

Fuck, was all Logan could think. She was right. As she always was. As only she could be.

Logan had screwed up royally. At least from this point out, he'd do his best to rectify his reputation with his former best friend, but he had no idea if it would possibly work. It was worth the effort, though.

Finally, he noticed the state of his clothes and body. Dried blood stained his right hand, the clothes he'd been wearing since Friday night stunk like the dickens, and a glimpse of his eyes he caught in the window looked more vacant than they'd ever been. He stared at himself for a good few seconds, disgusted at what he saw staring back at him, and then he left in a huff.

The steel door slammed shut one more time, leaving the heroic shot of Logan Ramsay in his Red Rider uniform as the only presence left. School would start in only a few hours, and he at least needed to get home and have a shower.

Chapter 9

Remade

The faint rumble of the morning freight train stirred Logan from the first sleep he'd gotten all weekend. Like many other Monday mornings, he'd overslept, and would have to sprint to make it on time for first bell. Sometimes he got privileges for being the coach's son, but mostly he was unwilling to accept them. He didn't particularly care for the attention.

Rushing down the sidewalk like two defenders were on his case, Logan peeled around the corner toward the brick building, nearly getting speared by a pick-up truck in the process. His calves burned with the power burst that gave him an edge over his adversaries, and his right foot clanked inside the doorway just as last bell sounded.

Late again.

He did his best to sneak into homeroom, but the teacher didn't even have to turn his head. "The bell already sounded, Mr. Ramsay," Mr. Matthew Briner said. Mr. Briner taught accounting, and had the roll of all his classes memorized, including this one. Nobody snuck past him.

"Sorry," Logan huffed, collapsing into his chair.

"I'm afraid that's one too many, Mr. Ramsay," Mr. Briner informed him. "Please go see Principal Solemekin. This kind of perpetual tardiness is unacceptable."

Sighing, Logan pushed back out of his chair and meandered down the hallway. The streamers from Friday's rivalry game littered the floor, half torn and shredded from the celebration. Soon it'd be time to put the new ones up for Massillon. *Next man up, next game up,* as his father would always say.

He knocked on the principal's glass window. "Mr. Solemekin?" he called.

"Mr. Ramsay," the young principal replied, opening the door. "We meet again."

"I'm sorry, sir," Logan said.

"We've had this meeting before, hmm? Have a seat, please."

Locking the door behind him, Mr. Solemekin paced behind Logan's chair before resting his hands on either side of him. "Wanna tell me what's going on?"

"With what?" Logan asked.

"Well, we could talk about this tardiness problem," Mr. Solemekin started, "or we could discuss what you were doing on the field last night."

Logan froze, both not wanting to be in trouble and not wanting to get Ellie busted, either. Mr. Solemekin released his grip, his leather shoes cracking each time he stepped on the shimmering floor. "School grounds are not public property when school isn't in session, Mr. Ramsay."

"I know," Logan admitted.

"Then what shall we do about this? Detention doesn't seem to work, and I wouldn't risk our star running back with that, anyway."

"That's fine if that's what you think is best."

"Nonsense. Just because you can't be responsible doesn't mean I'm going to deny the Red Riders a shot at the state championship. No, we'll need to find some sort of appropriate penance that doesn't affect your play on the field. We don't need your father upset at both of us when he comes back."

"It's really okay," Logan said, trying to get out of something worse, but the principal wasn't having it.

"Enough, Mr. Ramsay," he said. "Your father is risking his life for our freedom in the desert right now. The last thing he needs to be worried about is you. Would you stop being so selfish?"

"Selfish..." Logan repeated, trailing off.

"Yes, selfish," continued Mr. Solemekin. "A good boy would be working extra hard to make sure his father wouldn't have to worry about him. Doing work around the community, busting his butt on the field *and* in the classroom." He leaned on his desk, two fists pressing on the glass-top of the mahogany ensemble. "Think of your country, Mr. Ramsay. That's what your father is doing."

Logan couldn't take it anymore. He stood up, his chair flying back and crashing into the wall. The principal's secretary, Miss Isley, immediately opened the door, concerned.

"Mr. Solemekin, is everything okay?"

Mr. Solemekin didn't break the steely-eyed gaze he held Logan in. "Fine, Miss Isley. Please shut the door."

"But Mr. Solemekin…"

"Shut the door, Miss Isley," Mr. Solemekin gritted through his teeth. "Thank you."

Miss Isley looked around the room one more time, then reluctantly pulled the door back closed. Mr. Solemekin kept staring into Logan's eyes. "You got something to say to me, boy?"

"You don't get to call me 'boy,' sir," Logan said. "It's Logan, or Mr. Ramsay, if you prefer."

"That mouth is going to land you in bigger trouble than I can give you," Mr. Solemekin warned. "You're lucky I want the Red Riders to go undefeated, or I'd suspend you from all school activities myself."

"Do it, then." Logan stepped closer, refusing to back down. "What are you going to tell them? You kicked the coach's son off the team because he was late to homeroom? He wasn't there to immediately be counted for sitting around for twenty minutes until class actually starts? Oh, no, I missed roll call, how ever will my academic record be taken seriously again?"

"You've got an attitude problem," snarled Mr. Solemekin. "Maybe we should send you to boot camp too. That way, your father can keep an eye on you and the military can make you toe the line. We'll see how tough you are then."

"Can I go now?" Logan demanded.

"Get out," Mr. Solemekin muttered under his breath. "If I catch you on the field after hours again, I don't care what the ramifications are, you're gone. You got me?"

Logan slammed the door without a response, shaking the knick-knacks and picture frames nearby. Mr. Solemekin took in a deep breath, then realized his mistake and kicked his office chair.

"I forgot to punish him. Dammit!"

At the end of the school day, Bernie and Jimmy jogged toward the field door with Josh in between them, eagerly recounting the events of the weekend.

"You have no idea what Kathy can do," he proclaimed.

"Look at the freaking Casanova over here," Bernie said. "Got it in with Kathy in one weekend."

"As the kicker," Jimmy added.

"We went back to my place," explained Josh, "after the party at Coach's house."

"Yeah?" Bernie asked.

"Then what?" Jimmy demanded.

"We killed a bunch of zombies in *Resident Evil.* I've never made it that far on my own. She's better than I am on that thing!"

"If that's what you wanna call it." Jimmy smiled, taking it as a euphemism. Josh remained confused, as that was what really happened.

"Josh mackin' it, who would'a thought?" Bernie chuckled.

The three crossed paths with Logan. "Hey, Logan!" Bernie called. "Time to kick Massillon's ass!"

"And I'll kick the extra point when you score!" Josh added, trying to sound like the two but failing.

"Yeah." Jimmy tried to be enthusiastic. "The extra points... everyone's favorite part of the game..."

"See you out there, Logan!" Josh called as they partook in their pre-game rituals. Bernie and Jimmy put on their helmets and butted them against each other like giant rams. Jimmy turned to Josh and butted heads with him, and Josh flew back so hard that he flipped over himself.

"I'm okay!" he assured them, not realizing they had already sprinted toward the field.

"All right men," Coach Stewert proclaimed, doing his best Coach Ramsay impression. "We've got Massillon this Friday, and they have their sights set on the division championship too. They've beaten us three years in a row. Will anyone let there be a fourth?"

"No!" the Red Riders kneeling around him replied.

"Let's kick Massillon back down to the basement where they belong!" Coach Stewert paused, looking at Logan. "And let's win one for Coach Ramsay. On three, U-S-A!" One, two, three!"

"U-S-A!" the team responded in earnest patriotism.

Both doors inside the school crashed open as cleats pounding against the floor interrupted the afternoon silence. Logan thought he saw someone stuck behind one of them, and he stopped to take a gander.

"Get this thing off of me!" a voice called, finally pushing the door away from trapping them there. The door flew forward and knocked Josh back on his ass yet again.

"What a day." He got up and ambled along.

The echoes of cleats finally stopped pounding inside Logan's skull, and he turned to see Ellie walking away in haste. "Wait!" Logan called, though he wasn't sure why.

Ellie didn't stop, her skirt bouncing against her back. Logan trotted to catch up and peered over her shoulder. "Are you all right?"

"Fine," Ellie sarcastically remarked. "I always love

being trapped behind a heavy door when I'm trying to head to the office."

Logan was about to ask about the previous night when he saw Jimmy and Bernie at the end of the hall, waving toward him. "Hey, Logan!" Jimmy called.

"Yeah, come out with us!" Bernie chimed in.

As they jogged closer, their expressions suddenly changed to confusion. "What are you doing talking to *him?*" Jimmy accused.

"Her," Ellie corrected him before Logan could.

"What, you think putting on a skirt makes you a girl?" Bernie snickered. "You're still Ezra, and everybody knows it."

"You won't look like much of a man when a helpless little girl shoves her boot in your crotch," Ellie replied, her eyes turning toward Jimmy. "Though from the looks of you, that wouldn't hurt too much."

"You little..." Bernie started to advance, but Logan held out his hand to stop him.

"Knock it off."

"What are you doing, Logan?" Bernie asked. "This little fag's talkin' shit, and you're gonna back him up?"

"Her," Logan asserted. "And stop being an asshole."

"Okay..." Bernie stepped back, his hands in the air in a mocking gesture of peace. "Wouldn't want to interrupt your date or something. Come on down to Coachie's when you're done hanging out with the queer."

The two scampered away, Logan staring daggers at them the entire time. He turned around to say something to Ellie, but she was already headed out the door.

"Would you stop doing that?" he called after her.

Outside on the sidewalk, Logan again tried to get her attention. "Why do you keep walking away from me?" he demanded.

"Well, gee, Logan," Ellie snapped back, "maybe so I don't have to deal with that bullshit some more? If there's one good thing that came out of ditching football, it was losing that Neanderthal locker room talk."

"But I corrected them," Logan reminded her. "Right?"

Ellie finally stopped walking and put one hand on her hip. "Wow, congratulations, Logan, you did the bare fucking minimum and didn't misgender me one time. Good for you! Now that you've done your good deed for the day and decided to be nice to that tranny you know, you can go to Coachie's and yuk it up with those other jackasses."

"I'm not going to…" Logan started.

"I don't care," Ellie said. "Do whatever you want, I don't need your pity."

She turned and stomped away, leaving Logan in the dust. He wasn't sure what to make of it, so he sat down on the sidewalk, his legs splayed along the empty street, and stared off into the distance. Ellie, about a hundred feet away now, rolled her eyes and turned back around. Logan didn't notice until she was pulling him up by the arm.

"What are you doing?" he asked.

"I can't leave you there looking like a kicked puppy," she replied. "Come on."

"Come on where?"

"Come with me and you'll find out," she instructed, already a few feet ahead of him.

After about ten minutes of silence, Ellie disappeared behind a row of trees. "Come on," she called to him. "Keep up. You're a running back, aren't you?"

Logan ducked under a branch, a difficult task for someone his height. Leaves crunched under his sneakers, and twigs twisted and broke as he made his way through.

"What are we doing back here?" he asked, but received no answer. He followed the sound of her steps until he came to a stone path guiding some railroad tracks through a valley of autumn.

"This way," Ellie guided him from the other direction, balancing herself on one side of the rails.

"The train tracks?" he replied, concerned. "Are you sure?"

"Quit asking questions already," she insisted. "You're worse than my mother!"

A few dozen yards later, they were atop a bridge. He recognized it as the old stone arch outside of town. Ellie leaned against the side facing away from Orrville, looking off toward a parallel line that ran near an old salt plant.

"Out there," she said. "Private collector. Guy has several dozen old train cars, and even a few engines. He's taken me for a ride in them a couple times. One of them was back from World War II."

"Wow," Logan breathed. "I didn't know you were into that kind of thing."

She shrugged. "You never asked."

Logan shut up. He couldn't exactly argue with that. They hadn't spoken but once in about five years.

"Even before everything happened," she continued, "I've never been able to escape my fascination with railroads. I don't know what it is, especially with less obsolete forms of freight and transportation, even in this town."

"Yeah, I know the Volvo plant started using trucks," Logan agreed. "Took a huge cut out of one of the old lines. My grandfather worked there when he was young."

"They tear up old lines every year," Ellie said. "They disappear, or they turn into paths, or sometimes they just rot there, sinking into the ground, reclaimed by nature." She sighed, looking down at the street as a car passed under the bridge. "Nobody notices. Nobody cares."

"I think they do," Logan meekly suggested.

"You didn't until just now," she pointed out. "And you wouldn't have, if I hadn't taken you here."

"So what do you do here?" he inquired.

"Why?"

"I've never asked before. I'm asking now."

Ellie kicked a few stones, adjusting her hair so that it wasn't blowing in her face. "Sometimes, I don't know... It feels like I have a connection to it, like the way people see me."

"What do you mean?"

"Here's this thing, and it's been there, always. Then something else comes along, and it changes. People forget about it, they don't notice it. They let it fade from memory until it becomes invisible." She sniffled as a few tears escaped her eyes. "But it's still there. I'm still there. How much has to be lost of our past before they realize it's all gone? Will they even remember me if I'm gone?"

"I would," Logan said honestly.

"Oh, really?" She turned to face him. "What if I hadn't stopped you from doing something stupid last night?"

"I…" He stopped, knowing he was once again beat. Ellie definitely had a flair for seeing right through him like no one else could.

"Look, you gallivant around this town with your idiot friends, and nobody gives you any trouble," Ellie said. "You're late for the fifth day in a row, and you don't even get a detention."

He didn't understand what she was getting at. "So?"

"So?" Ellie repeated. "So? So if I use the bathroom, it doesn't matter which one I use—I'll be given shit for it."

"You will?"

"If I go in the women's room, like I should, there's always some douchebag there to complain that I shouldn't be in there with his girlfriend. And if I go in the men's room, I'll either be beaten up or groped."

"I'd never let that happen," Logan told her.

"How can you say that when you didn't know? I've been invisible to you for *years*. While your friends have beaten me up any chance they could, they're never punished for it because they play football in this stupid little town. After all, maybe I should just stop wearing a dress, be a man, and stand up for myself, right? Fuck you."

Ellie fell to the ground, leaning against the side of the bridge. She brought her knees to her face, hiding the tears streaming down in thick rivers now. Logan, still uncomfortable, sat down and tried to gently rub her back. She pushed his hand away.

"I'm trying to help," he pointed out, a bit hurt at yet another rejection.

"Logan," she sobbed, "I can't trust you." She lifted her tear-stained face up. Her foundation was starting to run, letting the mask she wore fade away little by little.

"Why now? You haven't given me so much as a thought since that day on the field. Why should you bother now? In a year, you'll be headed to Ohio State, or wherever else gives you the most money to come run a football for them. I'll still be here, dealing with the same townie bigots I always do. Forgive me if I'm not sold on your pity."

"It's not pity," Logan argued. "I didn't know any of this was happening, but I want to make sure it doesn't happen anymore. And why wouldn't you also go to college? You're smart. You work for the school paper. That should get you somewhere, right?"

"Oh, yeah," Ellie sarcastically remarked, "schools are just lining up to bring the transsexual girl in for an interview. Even if they do, they'll ask invasive questions, or ask what name is on my birth certificate, or worse, something about my genitalia."

"Your genitalia?"

"Yeah. I don't get why the first thing anyone wants to know about is what's in your underwear."

"Why? What is in your underwear?" Logan asked.

Ellie smacked him across the face, then pulled herself to her feet, storming off back toward the autumn valley.

"Ez... I mean, Ellie!" Logan called after her.

"Fuck off, Logan!"

Before Logan could get to his feet, she was gone.

Dammit, he thought to himself. *Why is she so easily offended?*

He did his best to shrug it off, but the uneasy feeling wouldn't leave him. Finally, he gave up on her coming back and headed home, sliding down the dirt next to the bridge and hitting the sidewalk with force. Lucky he didn't tear a knee with that landing.

He started walking back toward Kenwood Drive. He didn't much feel like Coachie's anymore.

Before he got to his front doorstep, he noticed an envelope stuck to the screen door. Darting up to see what it was, he saw the Army emblem on it, and his heart sank. Nothing left on your front door from the Army could ever be good news.

"Missing in action," Logan read out loud, his own tears starting to form. "Shot down, unable to locate at this time."

He dropped the paper, leaving it to flutter in the wind until it came to a rest on the giant rock in their front yard. He slid against the front door, coming to a sitting position on the porch. He'd never felt more alone in his life.

The pang of regret starting nagging even harder than usual, and the last thing he wanted was to be seen like this. He forced himself up, and slowly walked inside the house. He locked the door to make sure no surprises followed him in this time.

A red light blinking in the darkness caught his attention. *The answering machine*, he thought. *That's the last thing I need right now*. But the number "39" flashing repeatedly caught his eye.

"Some other time," he muttered out loud, before heading to his room. Maybe things would be better after some sleep.

What Logan didn't notice was Ellie standing at the end of his driveway, having collected herself, and watching the whole event unfold. Before she walked away, she saw the note slowly blowing down the lawn toward the street. Picking it up, her hand covered her chest as a gasp left her lips.

"Shit," was all she could muster. "Coach…"

Also knowing how Logan got sometimes, she pulled a pen from her bag and wrote on the back. "I'm here if you need me, you know where I am. —E." Then she re-taped the notice to the front door, and though she contemplated knocking, she opted not to do so. He knew where to find her, and unlike last night, he wasn't about to do something dumb. Something that would've broken her heart. Stupid feelings…

Chapter 10

Real

"Look at my weak, pathetic son," Robert Ramsay yelled through the shards of the television screen. Logan, pacing back and forth in front of it trying to plug his ears, refused to answer. "Answer your father and superior when he speaks to you, dammit!"

Logan stopped at attention purely out of habit and stared at the image of his father in combat fatigues. "You're not real."

"I'm not real?" Robert sneered. "You're the one bawling in the kitchen because I might be dead right now. Is that the sort of little bitch I raised?"

"I love you, Father! I could never lose you!"

"You make me sick," Robert taunted. "I should've pulled out instead of being stuck with someone who needs their hand held through life."

"You're all I have, Father."

"Not anymore. Now I'm probably dead in a ditch somewhere because I was too busy worrying about you. It's all your fault. You killed me, Logan!"

"No!"

"It's all your fault!"

"No!"

Logan collapsed to the floor and cried as the image of his father through the screen continued to blame him.

"It's all your fault, Logan. All of it. Everyone is going to hate you. They'll run you out of Orrville when they find out!"

"No!"

"Logan!"

A new voice, a different voice, interrupted the screaming match. Robert's voice stopped echoing throughout the previously empty house, and there were suddenly two arms wrapping around his stomach from behind.

"Stop it! Who are you?" Logan screamed, still in the desert somewhere being screamed at by his father.

"Logan," the voice tried to calm him, "it isn't real. You're safe. You're here with me. Your father doesn't hate you, I don't hate you. Come back to me now."

"Ellie?" he managed to eek out of the flurry of tears.

"It's me, your best friend, Ellie Crow," she replied. "Come back to me. I'm here. You're safe. I won't let anything happen to you. Come back to me."

The sand whirled into a fading mirage and became the carpet rubbing into Logan's cheek. As he regained awareness, he realized two arms really were wrapped around him on the floor. The hands sported painted purple nails, but possessed the strength of someone who could knock him flat on his ass at a full sprint.

It must really be her, he thought.

"There you go," Ellie soothed. "It's not real. It's all over. You're here with me, and I won't hurt you. Come on, back to Orrville, Logan."

His erratic breathing finally eased enough for him to suck air in. The television was still broken, but no longer was his father speaking to him through it.

The front door crashed shut from a strong burst of wind, and it startled him up into a sitting position. He panicked, but Ellie wouldn't let go.

"What is it, Logan? Tell me what it is."

"Sounds," he admitted. "The sounds. They're so loud."

"It was just the door shutting," Ellie explained as gently as she could. "Nobody's here to hurt you. Nothing's here to hurt you. I promise."

"But Father…"

"I know," she replied. "I saw the note. I'm sure he'll be okay. Now tell me about the sounds."

Logan unfurled his knees, opening like a wrapped Christmas gift, and his teary eyes finally met with his long lost best friend's. "Sometimes, things are really loud."

"What things?"

"Sounds," he explained. "Startling sounds, ones that I don't expect. They sound normal to some people, but they're magnified in my head. Fireworks especially. They blow up inside my ears and I can't hear anything. It sends me to that place."

"What place?"

"The place where everything goes wrong. The place where everyone hates me, where everyone left me, and where I can do nothing right."

"Is that where you go when you have episodes?"

"Yes," he confessed, realizing it was the first time he'd ever told anyone.

"Why didn't you ever tell me?"

"You left," Logan answered. "You left before I could tell you."

"When?"

"At the football field. I was trying to explain it to you."

"By calling me a fag, you were trying to explain it to me?" she sourly responded.

"No. See, this is what happens."

"What? When what happens? For the love of God, tell me, Logan!"

"When I try to tell people what it's like in my head," he continued, "I say the wrong thing. I get scared, and I see things."

"What do you see?"

"Everyone I love," he cried. "Hating me. Kicking me. Leaving me."

"Like your mom did?" Ellie asked.

Logan turned to her in a rage. "How dare you bring up my mother? Get the fuck out!"

"Logan!" Ellie screamed, refusing to be bullied. "Do you think this fear comes from your mother leaving you? Is it possible you think we'll all do what she did?"

"Leave me alone!" he yelled.

"That's it, isn't it?"

"Get out!" he bellowed again.

"I'm never going to leave you, Logan," Ellie replied, ignoring his demands. "I'm not going to walk out. I'm not like her, and your father is going to be okay."

Logan's brow furrowed and he sobbed, holding his knees and hiding his face between them. Before Ellie could comfort him, the door swung open again and Jimmy, Bernie, and Josh burst in with the girls following them. Erin, the last one in, grimaced at the sight of either Logan crying or Ellie being there; Ellie couldn't tell which.

"What the hell?" Bernie announced, coming upon the pile of broken dreams and deepest fears.

"What's... *that*, doing here?" Jimmy demanded.

"Logan, are you crying?" Erin asked. The disgust in her voice was palpable.

"Back the fuck off," Ellie snarled, rising to her feet and brushing the broken wood chips off her skirt. Staring down all six of them, she positioned herself between them and Logan, standing straight and not backing down an inch.

"Who are you to tell me anything?" Jimmy said. "You don't scare us. You're a freaking guy in a dress, you freak!"

"There's a thesaurus up in Coach's desk," Ellie snarkily replied. "Go ahead, brush up on your vocabulary. I'll wait."

Jimmy's face contorted in pure confusion. He turned to Bernie, who shrugged. Josh peeked up from behind Alice and Jamie.

"He's saying you're an idiot for using the same word twice in a sentence," he explained.

"Oh," Jimmy said. "Oh! Hey!"

"Look," Bernie cut in, "regardless of his way with words, you don't belong here. We do. Now get out of here before we embarrass you more than you already do yourself by wearing a dress every day."

"It's a skirt," Ellie corrected, "and none of you belong here."

"It's our coach's house," Josh insisted. "We have more of a right to be here than you!"

"None of you have a right to be here," Logan interrupted, silencing everyone. Nobody argued with the star.

"Logan," Bernie finally replied, sounding a bit hurt, "we're your friends."

"Do friends destroy houses?" Ellie asked. "Do friends make fun of their brothers when they receive the worst news of their lives?"

"What?"

"My father is missing," Logan said quietly. "They don't know if he's alive."

Their faces flushed in embarrassment, each of them looking at each other for the right thing to say. Erin tried to walk toward Logan to give him a hug, but Ellie stood directly in her path.

"Let me through. He's my boyfriend," she implored.

"I think you've done enough damage for one day," Ellie coldly asserted. She turned her head back toward Logan for confirmation, and got it from his nod. "Leave, all of you. And if I ever hear of you trashing Coach's house or hurting Logan again, you can all deal with me."

"This isn't over, hotshot," Jimmy warned. "You won't always have your boyfriend here for protection."

"She's not my girlfriend," Logan said to Ellie's utter dismay. She, however, said nothing as everyone filed out the door. Erin was the last to leave, glancing back up, forlorn.

"I'm sorry, Logan," she said. "Maybe we can try again

when you're feeling better." She slipped off the necklace she was wearing and let it drape off the banister before closing the door behind her.

Logan breathed in deeply, relieved to have all of them gone. It was a few seconds before he noticed Ellie's stare burning a hole through his chest. "What?"

"Are you that embarrassed of me, Logan?" she asked.

"What? I mean, no," Logan replied.

"Better point out that the tranny isn't your girlfriend to save face, right?" Ellie sneered. "Wouldn't want them calling you a fag too."

"That's not what I meant," Logan insisted. He reached toward her to touch her shoulder, but she brushed it aside.

"I don't need your pity," she said with a scowl. "I'll let you save face in front of the boys who clearly don't give a damn about you. Wouldn't want their opinion of the star running back to be tarnished, right?"

Logan stepped forward forcefully, grabbing Ellie by both shoulders. She struggled, but even her core strength wasn't enough to break the running back's grip.

"I'm not embarrassed of you," he said firmly. "This is what I mean, when things come out wrong. That's not at all what I meant. Please, listen to me!"

Ellie stopped struggling, but eyed Logan warily. "So you can say what you mean when you want to?"

He turned a sheepish shade of red, then released his grip, realizing she'd nailed him yet again. "I'm sorry."

"I know," she acknowledged. She then headed toward the door, to Logan's utter surprise.

"Wait, where are you going?" he called after her.

"I have homework to do too, you know," she

explained over her shoulder. "But I'll see you tomorrow morning?"

Logan was confused. "What's tomorrow morning?"

Ellie sassily put a hand on her left hip and flipped her hair. "What, you don't know you should walk a girl to school?" Her tone was facetious, putting a smile on Logan's face despite himself. "You owe me about five years' worth, anyway."

She opened the door, then curtly looked back once more. "Tomorrow?"

"Tomorrow," Logan affirmed."

She laughed "I'll be here to wake your ass up."

The door shut, and for the first time in a while, Logan didn't feel alone in his own house anymore.

Chapter 11

Walk

A pounding on the door awoke Logan from the best sleep he'd had in weeks. It was no longer a surprise to hear people coming into his house, as the team had been treating it like a hostel since his dad left. Groggily wiping his eyes, he grabbed a shirt and held it over his morning wood as he cracked the door.

"Hey, Ramsay," Ellie said. "Let's get a move on!"

Logan checked the clock. Late again, most likely.

"Hold on," he replied.

"I've been holding on for half an hour. Now I'm about to drag you out of there, no matter what you're wearing… or not wearing."

"No, no," Logan anxiously answered, "don't do that!"

The door swung open, and Ellie was dressed to kill. Wearing a long black dress and more makeup than usual, she stood in the doorway with a sarcastic smile on her face. "What, you watching porn or something?"

Logan sheepishly held the shirt over his boxers a little higher, and her gaze immediately snagged there. "Oh, don't act like I've never seen one before," she joked. "Or had one before."

Logan got uncomfortable at the mention of it, but Ellie didn't give him a chance to dwell. "Hey, suck it up," she laughed as she smacked him on the shoulder. "Your best friend's transgender. There, it's out in the open. We can all move on."

"No, we can't," Logan choked out. "We're late."

"Oh, that," Ellie snickered. "About that..."

"What?"

Ellie held up her pocket watch. "I sort of changed it yesterday," she admitted. "What can I say, I still know you better than anyone."

"So we're not late?" Logan inquired.

"Nope. You're awake on time for the first time since..."

"Ever," Logan finished for her. "I suppose I should thank you."

"Save it for when you need it," Ellie snarked, heading back toward the doorway. She looked back before leaving. "Take care of what you need to, whether that's just getting dressed, or... anything else."

His face flushed as red as his football jersey. Sure, it was Ellie, but still... Girls weren't typically prone to being that direct, at least as far as he knew.

Despite his reputation in Orrville, he'd never relied on favors in that department. He was always afraid of having an episode and ruining the entire thing, so it was better to avoid it altogether than risk town-wide embarrassment. He'd get to that, maybe at Columbus or something. At a school that big, nobody could know everything about everybody like they did here, right?

When Logan finally ambled out from his room, Ellie was eating from a plate of eggs in the kitchen. Another plate sat across from her, waiting for his attention.

"Hurry up," she instructed. "They're getting cold."

"You made me breakfast?"

She shrugged. "Don't flatter yourself. I got bored waiting for your lazy ass to wake up."

Ellie continued diving into her... damn, was that five eggs? Logan was mystified at her appetite. Where did it all go?

"So, you ready for the test from Mazaj?"

"That's today?" Logan incredulously responded.

"No," Ellie sighed, "but it doesn't sound like you would be if it was."

"Probably not," he admitted. Ellie had razor-sharp intuition, and there was no use in presenting the image he did with everyone else. She could see right through it, even after all this time apart.

"We'll study after practice," she informed him. "Can't have you falling behind and risking your ride to Ohio State."

"After practice?" he repeated.

"Well it's not going to be before," she laughed. "I know the routine."

"But..."

"Give it up, Ramsay. Whatever plans Beef Steak and Mutton Chop made for you can wait until you're back on track." She took a bite of her eggs. "Besides, I know you haven't been keeping up. That dazed look on your face might fool everyone else into thinking that you're with them, but I'm on to you, Ramsay."

She wiped her face and tossed the plate in the sink. "You done with that?" she asked, seeing that he hadn't touched it for a while.

"Yeah, sure," he replied.

"Good. We don't have much more time to waste."

The sidewalk seemed more comfortable with Ellie at his side, their steps nearly in unison just like old times. With the brick heights of Orrville High in the distance, the sun rose to greet them with a little extra warmth for that time of year. Or maybe Logan was just beaming at having a companion again.

"So, how are things at the paper?" he asked her.

"Same old," she responded. "Red Riders against Massillon, war, the protest, conservative talking points... Central Ohio."

"I imagine that can be frustrating," he replied.

"I doubt you'll have to worry your pretty little head much about it, darlin'," she cooed. "Politics don't matter when it comes to sports."

"More than you think," he countered.

"Oh? How so? Teams divide along party lines as well as mascot allegiance or something?"

"Well... no, not like that," he answered. "More like, those who are okay with... well..."

"Spit it out, Ramsay."

"With, you know, you... the gay thing."

Ellie stopped walking and tilted her head. "The gay

thing?"

"Yeah." Logan shuffled, looking down at the ground.

"What do you mean, 'the gay thing'?"

Logan kicked a stone toward the road, trying to avoid eye-contact. "It's cool, I mean…" He searched for the right word, unable to produce it yet again.

Before he could stall, Ellie pulled him back by the shoulder and held his face in her hands, forcing him to make eye contact with her. "Come on, say what you mean. I'm not going to freak out."

"Promise?"

"Promise."

Logan breathed a sigh of relief and stared off in the distance a bit, seeing the usual suspects gathering around the front entrance of the school. A few of them waved him over, but he held up a hand to indicate he'd need a few minutes.

"Hey, Ramsay," Ellie interrupted, "I'm not letting you off that easy. Say what you meant."

"Look Ellie," he stammered again, "I'll admit I don't get it, but I don't have a problem with it, either."

"With what, Logan?"

"You being… well, gay."

"I'm not gay, Logan," she firmly stated.

"But… the dress?" Logan again searched for the words, but came up empty, so he shrugged instead to indicate his confusion.

"What am I to you, Logan?" she inquired. "Be honest."

"You're Ellie Crow," he answered.

"I know that, but how do you see me? Like Beef Wellington over there?"

"No."

"Like Erin?"

"No."

"Then how?" She tapped her foot. "I'm not letting you go until you say it."

"I guess…" He trailed off. "With you dressing that way now, that was what I thought it meant. Becoming a girl and all."

"And as a girl, I'd have to be interested in other girls to be gay, right?"

"Yeah, but…" This was unfamiliar ground to him. She knew it, but wasn't letting him out the easy way. "When you became a girl…"

"Logan." Ellie grabbed him by the shoulders and pulled him closer. "I am a girl. I have always been a girl. You just didn't know that until I told you."

"Then what's the difference? Between that and gay?"

"What's the difference between my gender and sexuality?"

"Yes."

"Are you a man because of your interest in Erin?"

"No."

"Exactly," she pointed out. "Gender is internal. It's identity. Orientation is outward, expressive, attraction. I'm not gay because as a woman, I like to date men. I'm transgender, and I'm a straight woman."

"Sorry, I get confused," Logan replied. "It's just different, that's all."

"Think of it this way," Ellie began. "You had a best friend who was a girl growing up. If you'd never seen me any other way, like if I were just like Erin or something, would it matter?"

"No, I don't think so."

"There you go, then," she concluded. "Think of me like this, as I've always been inside. That's all you need."

"I think I get it," he said.

"Now go see your friends," she commanded. "I'll see you after practice."

Logan got through the day with surprisingly little hesitance. *It's nice,* he thought, *to not have to answer questions about my dad or Massillon for a change.* Go to class, go to the next, be a person. He could get used to that.

Erin avoided him at lunch, likely over what she'd seen back at the house. They'd been together for so long that he couldn't remember a time when they weren't, but maybe that was for the best. He could focus on football and his last year of school. Things that used to trigger his episodes were now rolling off his back like rain on a poncho. Awash in a sense of relief he'd long sought, he almost drifted through the day worry-free, and practice the same.

At least for most of it.

The two-minute drill was always the last part of Tuesday's practice. That was where they played full-on against the first-team defense with two minutes on the clock, like at the end of a half or the game. The offense would try to score, the defense would try to stop, and it ended the same way it would in a game: score, turnover on downs, or turnover from fumble or interception. It always fired up the boys at the end, making them look forward to the next game even more.

"Down by two, two to go," Coach Stewert announced. "Break!"

Logan pressed his knees in the backfield, waiting for the snap. He knew it was coming. Everyone knew it was coming. But could anyone stop him? Not often.

Hoying, the QB, dropped back, and then handed the ball to him. Draw play. Powering through the initial rush, Logan scampered down the line, going out of bounds after the first-down marker to stop the clock.

"Nice rush," one of the coaches called.

He felt glares penetrating his helmet from other directions, though he didn't have the time to stop and figure out why. He just repeated his father's mantra to himself: *Next man up, next game up. Let's go.*

Two plays later, after they'd gained another first down, Logan saw his chance to turn one up. Sweeping to the outside, the burst of speed for which he was known catapulted him over a linebacker, and he darted toward the end zone as he had so many times before.

Crossing into the painted red sod, he gently placed the ball down like they did in the old days and heard the whistle ending the drill.

"Offense wins," he heard coach announce.

Logan nodded back in that general direction, but suddenly...

Pow! A helmet-to-helmet spear from behind drove him into the turf like an undersized wide receiver. Teammates swarmed the incident on both sides, checking on Logan and pulling the culprit away.

"What the hell was that?" he heard one of the assistant coaches demand. "That's our star player, you asshole!"

"He's a fag-lover," one of them snarled in return. In his daze, Logan couldn't make out who it was, but it didn't matter. "We don't have room for queers on this team."

Continuing to shake off the cobwebs, Logan finally got up. Bernie and Jimmy were there, but didn't do anything to stand in the way either. Nobody did. It was Camponovo, the inside linebacker, who was hurling the accusations.

"We all saw you," he spat. "We all saw you with that queerbait. We don't need a running back who's into other dudes."

"Ellie's a girl," Logan stuttered, trying to fight a bad case of the spins. "And it's not like we're together or anything."

"Right, that's why she was over at your house with no one else home, you sick freak," Camponovo taunted. "We don't need you."

"Sit your ass down!" Coach Stewert interjected. "If I see anything like that again, I'll toss you myself!"

Coach pushed his way through to his star player. "Logan, are you concussed?"

"I'm fine," he lied.

"Your pupils are huge. Let's get you checked out."

He then turned back toward Camponovo. "That's your fucking teammate, you imbecile. He's the best chance we have at a state championship."

"Not if he can't keep himself away from the crossdresser," Camponovo laughed as he headed toward the locker room. Bernie and Jimmy looked back and just shrugged in response, also jogging off.

"Thanks, Coach," Logan mumbled once they were alone.

Coach grabbed him by the facemask and pulled him close. "Get your head in the fucking game, Ramsay," he demanded. "If you're doing something to piss off your teammates, this is what's going to happen. Knock it off, whatever it is."

"The team doesn't decide who my friends are."

"The team is who your friends are," Coach Stewert corrected.

"And I'm your running back," Logan growled. "If you want to beat Massillon, you're going to need me."

"Ohio State probably won't look too fondly on a running back with a healthy scratch in a division game," Coach informed him. "Choose your words and your friends a little more carefully next time."

Coach left him alone on the field, the sound of cleats hitting concrete disappearing with him. Logan knelt down in the end zone, trying to re-gather himself completely. *Who are they to tell me who my friends are?*

Once his eyes focused, he saw Erin standing against the bleachers with her arms folded. He nodded at her in a weak greeting, but she shook her head in response. Alice, Jamie, and Kathy gathered behind her, and she left with her back turned toward him like the team had.

What the hell is in the water in this town? he asked himself. Nevertheless, after years of being apart from the person he cared about most, he wasn't about to turn his back on her again. Maybe. He hoped. He didn't want to lose his status, either. As much as he liked to think it didn't bother him, losing it was a dramatic shift he wasn't sure if he was able to handle.

Damn Ellie. Why couldn't you have just stayed Ezra?

He hated himself for it, but a part of him couldn't deny that bit of resentment. Things would've been so much easier without that confusion, especially in this town.

Chapter 12

Confrontation

"I remember seeing these behind my grandmother's house," Ellie explained as they walked along an old rail line. It was obviously long out of service, with brush growing over the rails and some of the ties disappearing into the wet ground.

Logan kept pace with his hands in his pockets, making sure his feet landed squarely on every tie. Focusing on this prevented him from talking about what had happened earlier.

"Then, after she died, I had a feeling I'd never get back to East Fultonham, of all places, so I wanted to see the tracks one more time before we left the area. When we got there, they were pulling up the tracks. I started taking pictures of them because they'd never be there again, and neither would I."

Logan nodded, trying to understand her fascination, but ultimately distracted by other things going on.

"So that's when I started finding all the abandoned rail lines I could," she continued. "You never know when they won't exist anymore. So many stories exist on these rails, and I know so many people have memories like mine of their grandfather getting on the train and going to work. I don't want those memories to be lost like so many others, so I document them every chance I get."

"Uh-huh," Logan grunted.

"And then, once I take the pictures, I pretend to accidentally send them nudes to be crowned Miss America," Ellie said dryly.

"Yep," Logan replied, not turning his head or missing a beat.

Ellie smacked him on the shoulder, finally getting him to look up from his consistent downward gaze. "What the hell?" he hissed. "What was that for?"

"You weren't paying any attention to what I was saying," she snapped. "If I'm boring you too much with who I am, just tell me."

"I wasn't..." Logan stammered. "I mean..."

"What?"

"I'm sorry, something happened today, and I suppose it has me a little distracted." He stared off into the distance. With only trees in every direction though, his attempt to thwart the conversation wasn't going to work.

"What happened?" Ellie asked. "Tell me. I'm here."

"Well..." he began at length. "I sort of got knocked by a guy on the team, and every one of them and the coach seem to agree."

"Agree about what?" Ellie followed up.

"About... you," Logan replied, barely above a whisper.

"What about me?"

"They say that I shouldn't be on the team if I'm hanging out with someone… um…"

"Queer?" Ellie suggested. "Crossdresser? Tranny? Fag? What, Ramsay?" Ellie demanded his eye contact along with his attention. "What is it?"

He winced. "At least one of those. Even the coach criticized me for it.

"*Interim* coach," Ellie corrected. "Coach is your father, need I remind you."

"Coach Stewert is acting coach, and if my father doesn't come back, he'll probably remain there with the way the team is doing this year. Apparently, they have the influence to tell me who I should spend time with now, and I have no say in the matter."

"You always have a say in the matter," Ellie countered. "What are they gonna do, kick you off the team for hanging with a girl after the game?"

"I don't know," Logan muttered. "I don't know what to do."

Ellie gently stepped a few ties away, staring into the disappearing horizon of the fall dusk. "You don't know what to do?"

"I don't."

"Mr. Town Football Hero, who could get literally anything he wanted out of anyone in Orrville, doesn't know what to do?"

"Stop describing me like that," Logan replied in a whine. "It's not like that."

"Oh, of course it isn't," she bit. "This is the part where you break it off because it's easier to throw away the one genuine friend you have than admit you're hanging out with someone different and like it, right?"

Logan shook his head sullenly. "No."

"Wouldn't want the future Buckeye to be caught with someone who isn't a cheerleader, eh?"

"That's not it," he protested again.

"*I'm so sorry, Ellie,*" she said, mimicking his voice, "*but being seen with a trans person is too difficult for my reputation!*"

"Stop it, Ellie," Logan demanded. "I didn't say anything like that."

"You didn't have to," she replied. "I've heard it all before."

"Listen, please."

She finally stopped walking and stood near a particularly rusty section of rail. Her hand on her hip, she awaited the better part of the explanation. "Well?"

"It's just… look, I don't know how to explain to them that you're not Ezra."

"You tell them I'm not Ezra."

"Yeah, but they don't get it."

"Do *you?*"

Logan stopped dead in his tracks and stared her down. "What do you mean?"

"Do you understand it any better than they do?" she asked him.

"I guess," he answered, "I mean, I don't personally, but if you want to be Ellie, I don't see why it's an issue they need to be worried about."

"It's not," she replied. "It's not an issue you or any of them need to worry about or understand." She stepped off the rails into the grass, looking through the trees as if seeking a means of escape. "You don't have to get it, and I don't expect you to."

"But I want to, Ellie!"

"You can't," she said with a shrug. "You'll never get it."

"Then what can I do to help? Please, tell me."

"Answer me this," Ellie snapped, "Am I a girl to you, or just your old best friend in a dress?"

"Well, I mean, like, both, right?"

"Wrong answer!" she screamed. "I'm not some guy in a dress. I'm not a guy at all. I'm just like any other girl you know, and they wouldn't give you shit for hanging out with Erin or anyone else, so don't you dare try to break it off with me because they're giving you a hard time. I've been in those locker rooms. It's what those idiots do."

Ellie breathed in deeply, then sunk to her knees in the grass. Logan tried to help her up, but she swatted away his efforts. "Don't."

"Don't what?"

"I don't need your pity, Logan."

"Ellie…"

"What?"

"I'm trying, here!" he said, exasperated. "Give me a chance. I'm on your side."

Ellie's eyes met his. "Are you? Truly?"

"Yes!"

She rolled back her neck, feeling it crack in several places. Then, finally, she offered her hand to let Logan help her back up like he originally intended. He pulled her out of the muck, the mud staining her dress.

"Well, fuck," she snickered, "that won't be coming out anytime soon."

"Why didn't you change when you got home?" Logan asked. "I mean, I had practice and all, so you had time."

"I wanted to look nice for…" She trailed off, trying not to look at him anymore, but it wasn't working. "The walk. I wanted to look nice for the walk."

"Why? Do the abandoned rail ghosts have a fashion preference?" he joked.

"That's not funny," she responded.

"It kinda is," he said around a grin. Ellie couldn't help but laugh a little bit. That was easier than the real answer, after all.

"Logan, sometimes I swear you're the most oblivious person on the planet," she remarked.

"You're probably right about that," he admitted.

Back at his house on Kenwood, Logan sat on the barstool beside the counter, watching Ellie prepare a variety of vegetables to throw in with some steaks still in their packaging. She glanced back and saw Logan watching her.

"What is it?" she asked him.

"Nothing," he replied. "Just taking in the moment, I suppose."

"What moment?"

"I can't remember the last time someone made me dinner," he explained.

Ellie made a face. "Your dad didn't cook?"

Logan laughed. "If it wasn't microwavable, Dad was clueless with it."

"Don't you know anything around a stove?"

"Not really. But I know enough to get by."

"Not good enough," she responded. "Get over here."

"What, there?"

"Yes, here," Ellie insisted. "There's *oblivious* and then

there's *clueless*, Ramsay. Jesus."

Logan, abashed, slinked up to the side of the refrigerator.

"Get here where you can see, silly," she instructed. "There's nothing to be afraid of. I'm not going to turn you transgender by proximity."

"Can you do that?" Logan questioned.

"Oh yeah," she responded, laughing. "If you stand too close to us while we chop vegetables, the onion vapors make you catch the gay."

"Catch the gay?"

"Yep. Instead of crying, you start getting the incurable urge for anal."

"Ellie!" Logan cried, aghast.

"What?" Ellie feigned innocence. "Like you've never wondered."

"No, I…" Logan trailed off. "I never… I guess… I never thought you'd bring it up that way."

"I'm sorry," Ellie laughed. "I figured it was all you guys talked about in the locker room. That's everyone's biggest question though, isn't it?"

"About what?"

"About people like me, or about gay guys," she elaborated. "It's either our genitals or how we have sex that they want to know about."

"I mean, you don't have to…"

"I'm not ashamed of it, Logan," she replied. "You're the uncomfortable one right here."

"So then… like, how does it work?" he asked.

"Can you narrow it down more?"

"I mean, do you still…"

"Have it?"

Logan blushed. "Yeah."

"For now," she said. "I won't for much longer. The hormones made it essentially numb anyway."

"Really?"

"Yeah," she continued. "Made my drive go way down, and reduced the ability to cum."

"That sucks," Logan replied.

"Nah," she said, "I'd rather lose the ability to have sex the wrong way than deal with having it there the rest of my life."

"Then how do you... you know?"

Ellie laughed again. "You're so prudish, Logan. Are you a virgin or something? I figured you'd have the entire school slain by now."

"Yeah," Logan admitted in earnest. Ellie continued laughing, then stopped as she saw Logan's face not break out into some prideful smile like the other guys she'd known in the last couple of years.

"Wait, you're serious, aren't you?"

Logan nodded somberly. "I am."

"Wow, who would'a thought?" Ellie mused. "The star running back of Orrville High has never done it with a girl."

"Anyone," Logan specified.

"Oh, right, wouldn't want to offend your fragile masculinity," Ellie snickered.

"What do you mean?"

Ellie started to rise up, but realized he truly meant no malice. Cutting the final slice of a white onion then tossing it in the pan, she shook her head.

"You're full of surprises, Logan Ramsay," she finally murmured.

"So are you," he said.

"Oh?"

"Well, for one, you're making me dinner after all that's happened."

"Someone has to," she pointed out. "Microwave burritos won't keep you in good shape forever."

"Ellie, can you be serious for a minute?"

She shrugged. "I'm not Lance Storm, but I'll give it a shot."

"You don't understand," Logan pressed on. "Everyone talks about my father like I'm not there, like my only duty is to live up to his hopes, his dreams, his legacy. And now that he's missing, not only am I tired of only living in his shadow, but if he's gone for the rest of my life, that's who I'll be. Not Logan Ramsay, but Coach Ramsay's son. 'Oh gosh, I'm so sorry to hear about your dad,' they'll say. 'You should be so proud.' "

"You should," Ellie suggested.

Logan sighed. "Not the point, Ell. I know my father's a great man, and I know that he's serving his country, whether he's alive or not. But…"

"What, Logan?" Ellie inched closer, placing a comforting hand on his shoulder. "What is it?"

A tear escaped Logan's eye, and he tried to turn away, but Ellie wouldn't let him. "Talk to me, Logan. I'm here."

"I'm tired of not being allowed to have feelings because my father's so great," he confided in her. "Ever since he left, with everything going on, it's all about the military, 9/11, revenge—go, Army, go… But we're not allowed to be affected by it. We're not allowed to be sad because of it. That's selfish, that's greedy, that's not remembering what's really important."

"What *is* important, Logan?" Ellie placed her other hand around Logan's waist, trying to keep him from breaking down. "Don't you go having an episode on me. We're finally getting somewhere."

"I want to be a person in their eyes too," Logan explained. "Not just Coach Ramsay's son."

"You are," Ellie said, blushing a little bit. "You are to me, anyway."

"I am?"

"I'm making you a steak dinner despite everything that's happened, aren't I?" She smiled, gently motioning toward the pan. "I've never been above taking care of you."

Logan smiled too. "I appreciate that."

"Logan," she began, "you're not just Coach's son to everyone. You're more than that to a lot of people. Erin, the teachers, even the other teammates, though they're likely not bright enough to know the difference."

"How so?"

"At the risk of continuing this ego boost," she chuckled, "you're a leader. People look up to you. You may think they're looking past you to your father, but they're really looking at you."

"How? All they ever talk about is how I should be grateful for him," Logan muttered.

Ellie nodded. "Exactly. They're trying to keep you on that pedestal. Everyone's scared. They have been since last September. But you... you're the guy who has it all figured out. You're the big star, the one who's getting out of this town and not going down to the Smucker's plant to jar jelly for the rest of your life. If this image of you falls, then they have to look at themselves instead and regard their own fears."

"Why can't they do both?"

"People love to live vicariously," she answered. "Through celebrities, athletes, movie stars, musicians… That's what distracts them from having to answer their own toughest questions. That's why someone like me scares them too; they'd have to confront their own desires and deepest secrets."

Ellie turned with one arm to add some powder to the vegetables, but Logan gently grabbed her, turning her back. He couldn't believe what he was feeling at the moment with the atmosphere so quiet, so tender, so… right.

She slipped her arm back toward his waist and stared deeply into his eyes. Neither of them could deny the butterflies in their stomachs.

"Logan," Ellie whispered.

"Ellie," Logan repeated in return.

They slid a bit closer, but then… *pop!* Something in the pan reacted with the heat, and Ellie jumped back, startled.

"Goodness, I didn't realize it was that far along already," she blurted, finally ripping off the plastic from the steaks and tossing them in. The meat sizzled, and Ellie jumped again.

"Got caught up there a bit?" Logan observed.

"I suppose so," she agreed. "How do you like your steak?"

"Rare," he replied. "I like it still mooing."

"Good boy," Ellie said. "If you'd said well-done, I was going to smack you with a salmon."

"A salmon?"

"Seemed more effective than a raw steak." Ellie shrugged. "Go sit down now."

"But didn't you want me to watch and learn?" Logan protested.

"Go sit down," she repeated. "We already almost got in trouble once. Plus, we're too far along now to back up. Next time."

Logan slid over to the chair again, watching the master chef at work. "Next time?"

"Of course. I mean, if you want."

"I want," he said firmly.

Ellie turned her eyes back to the counter. They locked for a good, strong second before each of them looked away again, their tummies fluttering.

Logan noticed the framed picture of he and Erin from junior prom off to the side in the living room. He walked over while Ellie continued adding spices and held the frame in his hand. He barely recognized himself. He looked ridiculously uncomfortable in that teal tuxedo. Erin beamed, but Logan seemed so... vacant. So lifeless.

Was this what Ellie meant, he wondered, *about seeing right through me?*

Ellie turning over the steak broke his fixation with the picture, and after turning back to see the source of the noise, he placed the picture back on the wooden side table... then pulled it front-face down, leaving only his father's military picture standing up.

He rose, staring at the difference in the table's appearance with that modification. *What in the hell am I doing? What's happening?*

"Steak's done," Ellie announced, again breaking his internal monologue. He heard a plate slide across the marble counter and turned toward the first real meal he'd had at home since his mother left.

"Don't get too used to this," she joked. "I can't make steak every night."

"Aren't you going to have any?" he asked her.

"Yeah, making mine next," she said, "but had to make sure your teenage boy appetite was addressed first. Game week after all, right?"

"Right," Logan agreed.

Ellie turned to make the second steak, dropping into the sea of remaining grilled vegetables. She caught one last glance over her shoulder at the boy eagerly consuming her dinner and smiled. Then she turned toward her own meal preparation and shook her head.

No way in hell, she thought. *Just got caught up in the moment.*

Logan snuck peeks at her when she wasn't looking. She was doing her best to hide her blushing, but the redness was brought out all the more by her Red Riders hoodie.

Nah, Logan laughed internally, *no way was that more than a vulnerable moment from deep conversation.*

He caught one more look as she turned her own steak. He giggled to himself, finding the absurdity in the whole notion that something more was there. It was all just a misunderstanding.

Chapter 13

Reality

"My parents weren't really sure what to make of it back then, and I don't think they are now," Ellie explained. As she and Logan walked down the hall together, stares followed them like ghosts, but he only concerned himself with what she was saying. It was nice to be treated as a normal person and not given special treatment because of his father or the football he played. With Ellie, he was just Logan, and that was all that mattered.

"They're a bit protective, even if they don't get it though, aren't they?" he asked her.

"Understatement," Ellie giggled. "I fear for anyone who comes over."

"Was colder than an ice chest," Logan agreed.

Ellie stopped in her tracks and cocked her head. "How would you know?"

Logan realized he hadn't brought up the night where they were suddenly, and very physically, re-acquainted. "I stopped by looking for you a few days ago."

"Which day?"

"The day where you found me on the field," Logan said. "Or night, rather."

"You came looking for me when you needed help?" Ellie lightly touched her chest. "I didn't realize..."

"It wasn't a big deal," he replied. "It was just made very obvious that your mom was watching me and looking out for you."

"She didn't tell me you came looking for me," she mused. "I wonder what that's about."

"It was cryptic as hell," he said. "It was like she was sending a message without saying what the message was." He opened the door to the cafeteria for Ellie. The noise surrounded them, making it much more difficult to hear.

"What was the message?" she asked. She nearly had to scream.

"Don't fuck with my daughter!" Logan laughed.

Ellie playfully smacked him in the shoulder. "I can take care of myself."

Her gaze turned toward the tables where the football team usually sat. Her place in the high school hierarchy was well-known, so she didn't dream of asking this to continue.

"Go hang out with your friends, Logan."

"Are you sure?" He hadn't had any intentions of ending the conversation.

"I know who I am," she muttered, turning her head toward the back of the huge room, "and I know who you are too. Go, play, have fun. Let me know if any new analysis on the Cro-Magnon mating rituals are discussed."

"What?"

"Nothing, go," Ellie instructed before leaving for a different cafeteria line. He kept staring at her as she left, and she was quite aware of it. Finally turning around, and even blushing a bit, she waved him away. "Go!" she mouthed.

Logan approached the usual table with his tray. As he sat in his spot, all conversation around him ceased. Oblivious to social cues as per usual, he barely noticed. But then, without hesitation, the team rose in unison and left him there alone.

Weird, he thought. *Must still be about that stupid shit from last practice.*

Logan continued eating by himself at an empty table. The quiet was kind of nice, really. He started mulling over one of the books in his bag that Ellie had recommended earlier, and lost himself in the pages of Kurt Vonnegut.

Eyeing him from a back table, Ellie couldn't let him sit there like that. After a few minutes of no change in the antics of his teammates, she sighed, got up, and walked across to the Forbidden Lands. Pulling on the sleeve of his jacket, she broke his concentration.

"What are you doing?" he asked.

"Come with me," she said, pulling him to his feet and making him to drop his book. He picked it up, then barely resisted being dragged along.

"Where are we going?"

"I'll be damned if I'm gonna watch you eat there, sad and alone," she responded.

"I was fine," he countered. "I had a book."

Ellie pulled Logan onto the double seat at her table,

and several other unfamiliar faces looked back at him with expressions ranging from contempt to apathy.

"Here, sit with us," Ellie insisted. "Nobody's gonna get up and leave because you're seen talking to me here."

"We might for other reasons," one of them snapped. Logan couldn't tell if it was sarcasm or not, and the raven-haired girl in fishnets quickly confirmed, "That was a joke, Ramsay."

"Hey," Ellie said, "nobody calls him that but me!"

"Man, your girl's so defensive," a rather flamboyant guy teased. "Guess there go my chances."

"She's not my girl," Logan replied. They all looked at him strangely.

"Then what are you doing here?" the first girl inquired. "Ellie's never brought anyone over here before."

"I'm Logan," he said, reaching across the table. The girl timidly shook his hand.

"Eliza," she finally replied. "And that's Lucinda, Noah, Heath, Eli, and Sarah." Going down the line, he acknowledged them all with a polite nod.

"That doesn't answer the question, though," Eliza chastised.

Logan blinked. "There was a question?"

"What are you doing over here?" Noah asked. "Isn't this the table of the invisibles for you?"

"The invisibles?"

"The Island of Misfit Toys, so to speak," Eli, the flamboyant one, followed up. "The star football players aren't usually caught dead with us."

"Except for Josh," Heath added.

"Yeah, but Josh hasn't been around since he became the kicker," Sarah chimed in.

"Guess he finds the allure of Bernie and Jimmy much more interesting," Ellie cracked.

"Maybe if you can get past the body odor," Eli teased. "No offense, Logan."

"You mean you guys don't like them, either?" Logan asked.

Everyone, including Ellie, stared at him in disbelief. "Are you serious?" Heath said.

"Yeah."

"Logan," Ellie said gently, "they're sort of responsible for tormenting the entire school."

Each one of them nodded coldly. Logan recalled earlier in the year when Ellie had stopped his friends from turning Josh into a chew-toy.

"Have they always been that way?" he asked.

"Always," Noah confirmed.

"Since the first grade," added Eli.

"I never knew that," Logan muttered.

"You're probably under the same false impression that the jocks run the school and can do whatever they want," Ellie informed him. "I've been there."

"I've never done anything like that to you," Logan said, then looked around to the rest of the table. "To any of you, right?"

They all shook their heads. "But you've never stopped it, either," Eliza supplied.

"I would have," Logan said, "if I'd known about it."

"Would'a, should'a, could'a," Eli groaned.

Before Logan could find out more of what he'd been missing, another young guy dressed in flannel with thick-glasses darted toward the table. "Guys! Guys!"

"What is it?" Ellie responded with a bit of fear in her

voice.

"The church, they're protesting outside," the kid explained, out of breath.

"*That* church?" Eli inquired, with an extra sneer.

"What church?" asked Logan.

Ellie patted his arm. "I gotta go." She stood up, but Logan rose with her.

"No, I'm going with you," he insisted.

"Don't get yourself involved with these guys," warned Ellie.

"What?" Logan asked. "I go to church. What's the problem?

"It's not that kind of church," Eli muttered.

Logan heard the megaphone before he saw the source. The words on the sea of poster boards and picket signs weren't clear, but the intent was unmistakable.

"Are we going to continue to let this indoctrination take place in our public schools?" the man on the bullhorn asked.

"No!" several voices shouted back.

Logan slipped his way through the crowd into a circle of people. In the center of them, a balding, middle-aged man was shouting into a megaphone and sporting a t-shirt that read "homos." A red "X" struck out the word.

"The devil is working his fingers through the very fabric of our society when queers and fag-lovers can run free in the school without consequence!" the pastor continued. "We must insist that the Bible be used to show these children the way before it's too late!"

"Hallelujah!" one woman called out.

"Amen!" another agreed.

"If we continue to let the good, godly children of Orrville High suffer under the name of 'tolerance' and 'diversity,' then the whole lot of them will suffer the same fate as Sodom and Gomorrah! This kind of political correctness will not be tolerated!"

Logan inched closer to the pastor. The pastor, noticing him in his Red Riders letter jacket, pulled him closer for visual effect, making him very uncomfortable.

"Do you see this good, young, Christian boy?"

"Yes!" several of them answered.

"This is the example of the child we should be encouraging, instead of the queers, fags, and feminists that have taken over!"

"Shove it, you antiquated dickweed!" Logan knew that voice, and smiled in response.

Ellie stepped forth, to the awe of even the popular kids standing around the confrontation. Logan pulled his jacket away from the pastor, to the man's visible dismay.

"Excuse me," the pastor hissed, curling his lip, "but we don't allow boys dressing up as girls to participate in discussions about God's word! Demon seed!"

"From what I understand, you don't allow women to participate in anything at all," Ellie replied. "Unless they're barefoot and pregnant and serving your whims, am I right?"

"The Bible specifically states the role of a woman in a heterosexual Christian marriage," the pastor shouted back. "And nowhere does he mention that a boy can become a girl if he wants to!"

"I don't recall it mentioning anywhere that bringing your fucking religion onto public school grounds is something you should do, either!" Ellie screamed, growing red and exasperated as she did so.

"Young man..." the pastor started.

"*Her* name is Ellie," Logan interrupted. A cold silence washed over the circle, with some of the supporting church members muttering in disgust, but the rest of the school watching on to see where this was going.

"Young man, I don't think your father would be proud of you openly defying the Lord this way," the pastor warned.

"I don't think my father would be proud of you putting words in his mouth," Logan argued back, and audible cheers sprang up from the students.

"Disgusting," the pastor growled. "The devil has gotten to this one. What a shame for a nice-looking young man to be taken in by the lies and deceit of homosexuality!"

"How is it homosexuality if she's a girl and he's a boy?" Eli yelled from a few rows back.

"And how is it any of your business, even if it was?" Eliza called from a different side.

Logan smirked at the pastor. The pastor then grabbed the lapel of his letter jacket and pulled him close.

"Your father is out fighting for our country in the name of God right now, and he's thinking about how he's going to burn in Hell for raising such a despicable son. In fact, he's probably already dead and burning now out of being ashamed."

"What did you say?"

"Apparently, this boy has not heard the word," the pastor proclaimed.

"Don't," Logan warned.

"We all love Coach Ramsay, don't we?" The pastor

received more cheers for mentioning the name of the beloved coach. "He's out fighting in the name of God against the people who killed so many on 9/11, is he not?"

"Don't do it," Logan more aggressively cautioned him.

"Well, folks, I've got some bad news for ya." The pastor grinned as he shot Logan a look of utter disdain. "Coach Ramsay is dead."

"What?" Horrified gasps sprang up from the crowd, and Logan's face turned white.

"You all have been in school, and if you'd been allowed to pray like you should, maybe you would've gotten the news already," the pastor mocked. "But since God's not allowed in schools, let me tell you in the name of God right here, right now, that Robert Ramsay is dead."

"No, he isn't," Logan meekly protested.

"How *dare* you?" Ellie gritted.

"He's dead and burning in Hell out of being ashamed of his fag-loving son!" The pastor got up in Ellie's face this time. "You disgust me, you sick freak. You should be electro-shocked until the word of God can reach you before you ruin any other lives."

"The only life ruined here is anyone who is dumb enough to listen to your self-righteous bullshit," Ellie fiercely replied. "Robert Ramsay is *not* dead."

"Yes, he is," one of the church members called back. "And he's burning in Hell."

"Sinner!"

"That make you mad, boy?" The pastor teased Ellie, and then he pulled on her blonde hair. "Why don't you take off this wig, you pathetic homo!"

Logan grabbed the pastor's wrist and flung him back,

sending him sprawling. "Don't you ever touch her again, and if I ever hear of you speaking of my father again, I'll come after you myself!"

A cheer arose from the majority of the students right before Mr. Solemekin got through the crowd. "What is the meaning of this?" he demanded. "Why aren't you all in school?"

The pastor got to his feet, dusted off his jeans, and tried to regain his composure. "We're trying to save your school, Mr. Solemekin."

"Far as I can see, the only thing you're doing is putting your hands on my students!" Mr. Solemekin accused. "I may not particularly care for the decisions of some of them, but you're a grown man! You have no right to be here, and no right to touch one of my students, you son of a bitch!"

Several "oohs" echoed through the crowd of students, and Logan's jaw fell slack.

"I pay taxes, so I have more right to be here than any of them!" the pastor claimed.

"This is a public school," Mr. Solemekin informed him. "Religion has no place here."

"And that's why all your children are falling under the corruption…"

Wham! Mr. Solemekin's fist collided with the pastor's mouth. A brawl broke out between the two of them, with Logan and several others trying to separate everyone. A few of the football players and teachers managed to get Logan away with both arms secured, but Ellie was stuck in the mix.

Logan spotted her fall down, and he begged, "She's trapped! Let me go! She's on the ground!"

"We got this," a familiar voice assured him.

A wave of surprise caught Logan in the tide. "Josh?"

Coach Stewert and Mr. Briner each had arms around Ellie as students divided to let them through. Her eye was bruised, her lip was bleeding, and dirt and scrapes covered both her legs. Logan struggled until the two other players let him go, and caught her as she was about to fall.

Police sirens interrupted the moment, and students and church members alike scurried away. Logan held Ellie in his arms as Mr. Briner tried to signal one of them. "She's hurt! We need help over here!"

Logan looked at him in complete shock. Coach Stewert rubbed his shoulder to comfort him. "I'm sorry, son. We got your back."

The pastor and Mr. Solemekin were both being led away by several cops. The pastor connected eyes with Logan, and smiled. "Your father died because you're a fag, Logan! The devil has cursed you all!"

Mr. Solemekin gave Logan a sympathetic look as he was being cuffed, just before one of the police officers helped him duck his head into the police cruiser. Josh came back with an ice pack and handed it to Logan.

"We're sorry, Logan," Josh apologized.

He stared at them. "For what?"

"For turning our backs on you," Josh replied. "Coach would've never wanted that."

"Is it true?" Logan inquired. "What they said?"

Josh sighed as Coach Stewert shook his head. "They don't know," he explained, "but it doesn't look good. The rest of his unit was found, but your father wasn't recovered."

"Found?" Logan asked for confirmation.

"Dead," Coach Stewert clarified. "His unit was taken out. He's the only one MIA, and I'm afraid that's the only conclusion to which they've been able to come. Have hope, but know that the news may not be good, son. I'm so sorry."

Logan's walls started breaking, and Ellie tried her best to comfort him, but she was too weak to grasp anything. Logan started to fall, and Coach managed to grab Ellie in time before she collapsed with him.

Logan stared into the sky as his teammates surrounded him. They were no longer his teammates. They were garbed in Army helmets and fatigues, and an explosion sounded in the background. One of them screamed, "Incoming!"

They all covered their heads, and an explosion sent several of them flying. Logan, after uncovering his own face, crawled over to the closest body he could find. "Are you okay?" he screamed over the noise.

He pulled the body over to face forward, and it was his father. Logan dropped him in horror and backed away on his knees. His father's face fell open, blood gushing, his eyes completely gone. Then he disappeared into the sand, leaving only bloodstains that slowly began to spell out, *It's Your Fault.*

Logan screamed at the top of his lungs, tears running down his face.

"Get him help!"

Coach Stewert and several more teammates were desperately trying to hold back an out-of-control Logan, but even most defenses had problems doing that. He broke free of Coach and then plowed right over Josh, sending him flying back into the mulch near the wall, and sprinted to the center of the grassy field in front of the school. He dove to the ground, rose to his knees, and then began screaming.

Josh tried to run after him, but Coach held him back. "There's nothing we can do."

Logan's vision finally spotted the huge red flag dangling over the field that was clearly not a desert. Tears streamed down his face as he hyperventilated.

Suddenly, the flag began lowering. Logan stood up, not believing what he was seeing, and his teammates followed his stare. It stopped halfway, and a blanket of sadness covered everyone standing there as they realized what was going on.

Ellie tried to stand up, but one of the police officers treating her wounds didn't allow her to move. "Stay put," he instructed gently. "We've got to get you cleaned up."

"Logan..." she whispered.

"Don't worry about him," the officer replied. "We're all here now."

Logan's eyes darted around, seeing the aftermath of the mess that had transpired. Noticeably absent from all the melee were Bernie and Jimmy, but a majority of his fellow Red Riders stood by, protectively surrounding Ellie and Josh.

Logan staggered back toward the group, heading toward the building. Several of his teammates stepped forth and gave their condolences in the form of hugs and shoulder taps. Logan tried to move toward Ellie, but Coach Stewert pulled him away.

"She'll be okay," he insisted. "We won't let anything happen to her again."

Chapter 14

Defense

"**D**ouble-option on two, on two. Ready, *break!*"
Logan left the huddle, trying his best to keep his focus on the Massillon defense. They were fighting hard, and even playing a little bit dirty, so he needed to be on his game. This was no time for visions; he needed to play well like his father would've wanted.

"Hut one, hut two," the second-string quarterback, Vincent Heathers, called before taking the snap. Vincent took off to the right with Logan trailing behind him, then flipped the ball back near the corner.

One Massillon defender swiped by in front of him, then put on the jets and darted along the sideline for a first down. He stepped out of bounds, then was hit by two Massillon linebackers dead-on. The crowd broke out in cheers, being the loyal Massillon fans they were, and the defenders got in some cheap shots before the refs pulled them off.

"That's a late hit, ref!" he could hear Coach Stewert screaming from the sideline. "He went out of bounds before they even touched him!"

The ref nearest to him ignored the accusations, and the coach threw his headset down in disgust. Then a flag flew up in the air, and the crowd descended into further madness.

"Unsportsmanlike conduct, Orrville sideline, fifteen-yard penalty!"

"Are you fucking kidding me?" Coach Stewert raged. The head ref then ran over and threw the coach out of the game.

In the third quarter, with the game tied, the crowd was in a frenzy, and Logan was bruised to hell on his ribs.

Signs in the crowd aimed at Logan let him know exactly what the Massillon crowd thought of him. "No Gay Buckeyes!" one said. "Smear the Orrville Queer!" another read. None of it was subtle.

Finally reaching the huddle fifteen yards from the spot of Logan's last run, Vincent was terrified. "They're all over us, man!" he whimpered. "And the refs are letting them do it! What do we do?"

"Give me the ball," Logan demanded.

"Are you kidding?" Vincent replied. "They're hitting you harder than anyone!"

"Well it's about time someone started hitting back," Logan muttered, and they called break.

The boos and chants were deafening. Everything started going into slow-motion for Logan again. He turned his head to the sideline for the call, but there his father was. Suddenly, nobody else was in the stadium, and his father grew younger before his eyes. They were back in Orrville, tossing the ball in the cemetery.

Young Logan's hands dropped a pass to the ground, even with it being right to his center. He groaned, sinking to his knees, and smacked the ground in frustration.

"Get back up!" Coach Ramsay called. "Get up right now! Ohio State needs running backs who can catch too!"

"Sorry, Coach," Young Logan responded.

"Don't apologize, stop being so worried. Nobody's here, just you and me buddy."

"And me!" A familiar voice added. Well, a voice that used to be familiar, anyway. Ezra darted between the two.

"And Ezra," Coach echoed. "But he'll always be here, won't you?"

"No matter what," he replied.

Logan then heard the current voice of Ellie talk over that vision.

"No matter what," it repeated, but in the voice of the girl he knew.

The two disappeared into the blue and yellow streamers of Massillon again, and the center was calling the play. Vincent snapped it, and before he could even turn around to hand him the ball, Logan took it and ran straight at the line.

The tackles pushed two big defensive ends out of the way, and Logan took off. Scurrying around two more diving linebackers, the only one remaining was the strong safety, who had left a welt on his cheek earlier in the game.

"I've got you now, faggot!" he proclaimed, then dove for Logan's knees.

Logan timed it just right so that when his facemask came near his legs, his knee jutted him right in the face.

The safety never got any hands on him, and Logan sprinted toward the end zone untouched the rest of the way.

He spiked the ball and turned back around with his arms open, like local celebrity LeBron James would often do at basketball games. Several Massillon defenders hustled toward the end zone, their plans made perfectly clear by earlier actions. Before they made it, Orrville players from the bench got in formation across the end zone and stopped their targeting. When they tried to pass, they were held at bay.

"We'll get you next time, Ramsay!" one of them threatened.

"You won't always have this much time to have your Orrville homos stand up for their little bitch!"

Logan trotted toward the Orrville sideline. Security was growing thicker between the Orrville stands and the field, mostly due to the objects being thrown in their direction from the track.

"It's like a riot out here," Logan mused out loud, not realizing he was right next to Bernie and Jimmy.

Bernie grabbed him by the shoulder pad. "Yeah, and it's all because of you," he sneered.

"What?"

"You and that little cunt," Jimmy followed up.

Logan's eyes darted to each side, looking for help, but it didn't look like anything out of the ordinary. "You may have all of them fooled," Bernie whispered, "but we know the truth."

"They only stood up for you because of your dad," Jimmy added. "And once he gets back, he'll whip your little faggot ass back into shape. That is, if Ezra doesn't do that first."

Logan shook off their grip and stomped back toward the sideline. Even with his strength, he couldn't take on both of those mammoth defensive players. "Just do your job!" he heard Jimmy yell.

But it was Bernie who got the last word. "And quit being a bitch!"

Logan watched on. The game was tough, tight, and close. With Orrville holding on to its lead late in the game, Massillon drove the ball into Orrville's red zone. It took sixteen plays, so the defense was wiped, especially because Massillon's runs kept them from substituting out as often.

They broke huddle at the eighteen and handed off to their speedy tailback. He ran straight at Bernie and Jimmy, who moved toward him for the tackle, but then let him run right by. The tank they pulled distracted everyone else, and the crowd erupted as Massillon tied the game.

Bernie and Jimmy removed their helmets and jogged off the field with smiles as Massillon set up for the extra point. Coach Bosnick, filling in for Coach Stewert for the remainder of the game, demanded to know what the hell all that was about. The two fist-bumped and ignored his call, and Coach Bosnick kicked the ground in frustration.

"We've got less than three minutes left," Coach announced. "If this goes to overtime, it's anyone's game. But we've got the ball, and they know what's coming. Make something happen. Do it for Coach Ramsay!"

"Coach would be disgusted with this," Bernie laughed.

"Did I fucking ask you, son?"

"No, but maybe you should ask the fag-lover over

there," Jimmy suggested.

Coach stood firm. "Either you two knock it the fuck off, or I'll toss ya from the game myself."

They shrugged. "Fine by us."

"Fine, get the hell out of here. If we get back on defense, we'll play the frosh."

"Me?" Josh pointed at himself in terror.

"You're all we got left. You and..." Logan knew where the Coach's gaze was coming next. "Logan, you ready to step in? All our other defenders are injured. You're the best chance we've got."

"Are you serious, Coach?" Bernie asked incredulously.

"Get the fuck off my sideline before I throw you off the team!"

Bernie and Jimmy both locked eyes with Logan, but their threats were masked by a cheer coming up from Orrville's section. They'd returned the kickoff for a touchdown to take the lead! 78-21, 2:43 remaining, Orrville in the lead. Logan and Josh each glanced at each other, obvious and overwhelming terror in their eyes.

Coach grabbed each one of them by the facemask. "You two are the best chance we have. Those dirty motherfuckers have taken out all our reserves. You're gonna have to Iron Man this shit, you got it?"

"Coach, I'm a kicker!" Josh protested.

"I know. Now get in there and kick the extra point before I do it myself!"

Josh scurried out onto the field just in time for the whistle to blow. Delay of game; it took too long.

"Five-yard penalty, repeat kick," the ref informed the crowd.

Josh looked back, shaking in his helmet. "Kick the ball, dammit!" Coach Bosnick screamed. The snap came back, but before Josh could kick it, the Massillon D-Line knocked the ball out of the punter's hands, plowed through Josh, and ran it back for two points! 27-23!

Logan fearfully glanced at Coach. Coach didn't return the gaze, but knew its context.

"Kid, we lose the shot at states if you guys blow this. Now with a touchdown, they'll probably win." Coach turned toward him finally, revealing a military patch under his polo sleeve. "Get them for your father, for your country, for your teammates, and for your girlfriend."

"She's not my…"

"Whatever, kid. Just fucking do it! One time!"

Josh's kickoff went out of bounds, giving Massillon the ball at the forty-five. None of the Orrville players could hear themselves think over the noise of the hometown crowd. Amidst their screaming, Logan helped Josh over to the right position.

"Stay back in the safety spot," he instructed.

"Which one's the safety spot?" Josh asked.

"Back there!"

Snap! Massillon's tailback cut through the line and ran right at Logan. Logan showed terrible form, but managed to run him out of bounds at the other forty-five, a first down for Massillon.

"I'm coming for you," the tailback warned, "and then I'll make your boy my bitch!"

Logan attempted to go after him, but a few of the Massillon players prevented him from doing so. "Don't even think about it, bitch!" one of them teased. "Or is your boyfriend the bitch?"

Logan glared intently at the tailback, who pointed right at him. The next snap flew back, and it was a play-action pass to the same tailback. Logan tried to chase him, but was planted from behind by a Massillon blocker. He couldn't bear to look up until he heard a shocked gasp.

Turning his head, he saw Josh with the ball! The ref whistled and pointed in his direction! "Fumble recovered by number one, Orrville ball!"

The Massillon crowd nearly broke into a riot of their own. Chants of, "Bullshit!" drowned out the outnumbered Orrville fans, but security covered the field immediately, preventing any action from taking place.

With no time-outs remaining, Massillon couldn't stop the clock. The game was over. Orrville was going to the district final, once again against rival Wooster, whose only loss came against Orrville that very season.

"Final score: Orrville 27, Massillon 23," the PA announcer, barely audible, reluctantly informed the crowd. The Red Riders picked Josh up over their heads and carried him off the field toward the visiting team's locker room.

"How the hell did that happen?" Logan wondered aloud before the coach slapped him from behind.

"Josh put his head into the ball," Coach Bosnick replied, dragging him along for the victory jog. "At his height, it was the only defense he had!"

On the bus, Logan tried to stretch out, but these seats weren't made for people his size. Everything hurt worse than normal, and the rest of the team must've felt similarly judging by the collective groaning.

He leaned his head against the window and tried to

fall asleep on the way back home, but there was a tap on his arm.

"I was supposed to give this to you," one of his teammates whispered.

A note. He unfolded it and tried to hold it under a passing street light. "Meet me at the cemetery. —E," it read.

Weird, Logan thought. *She's not going to just wait for me? Oh, well.*

The bus arrived, and the bruised, battered, but nonetheless victorious Riders shuffled off. After changing clothes, Logan headed back up the road toward the cemetery he'd envisioned earlier that evening. Maybe he'd visit his grandfather before Ellie got there.

"I'm so proud of you," Ellie proclaimed, hugging him around the neck. "And I know your dad is too."

"Could we not talk about him?" Logan requested, gently removing Ellie's hands from his neck. Not because he didn't appreciate the hug, but everything hurt.

"Logan," Ellie replied, "he's proud of you, no matter where he is."

"I'm sure," he snapped, "but I don't need to be reminded of it right now."

"Reminded?"

"It's hard enough getting killed out there by those guys, especially when they're getting away with it. The last thing I need is to be reminded of my father, who's probably dead in a desert somewhere."

"I know it's tough," she began.

"No, you don't!" Logan screamed. "You have no idea what it's like!"

Ellie dropped her hands and stepped back. "I don't

know what it's like…" she repeated under her breath. "I don't know what it's like."

"No, you don't!" Logan confirmed, though in a softer tone this time.

"All this time," Ellie replied, "I thought you might've been paying attention, but clearly you can't even see outside yourself."

"What the hell does that mean?" Logan demanded.

Ellie reached into the front of her shirt, pulled something out, and threw it at him. It bounced softly, but still caught him by surprise.

"What the fuck?"

"You think you're the only one with problems?" she sneered.

"What?"

She thrust something in his face. It seemed soft, like a tiny couch cushion.

"What is that?" he asked.

"That's my boob, Logan," she answered.

Logan looked down at her chest, which now barely showed two bumps. Ellie pushed him back, catching him off guard and sending him onto his butt.

"Those are my boobs, Logan," she shouted again. "That's what I have to do before I leave every morning!"

"Why?" he asked.

"Because the hormones haven't quite given me the obvious chest I need yet," Ellie cried. "The facial hair is gone, but my jaw is still way more masculine than I'd ever want it! And the boobs haven't grown like the doctor said they would! And the hormones mess with my appetite, my tolerance, and my moods!"

"Obviously," Logan mistakenly replied out loud.

"Wait, I didn't mean that!"

"You meant every word," Ellie muttered. "You don't give a shit about anyone but yourself and your own goddamn problems."

"That's not true," Logan protested.

"Yeah?" she asked, turning around and looking over her shoulder. "Then why didn't you kiss me the other day?"

"What?"

"The other day," she reminded him, "when I was teaching you how to cook. Why didn't you kiss me?"

Logan stammered. "I... um... I didn't..."

"You were too worried about what everyone else would say if you were dating a tranny," Ellie filled in for him. "Well, forgive me, but I'm not your fucking charity case. I'm not wasting any more time on someone who only cares about himself."

"Ellie, wait!" he pleaded.

"I waited long enough," she responded as she disappeared into the darkness.

Logan tried to follow her, but lost her in the night. He couldn't believe it, but it felt like his heart was breaking. How did this happen? How did it get to this point? How did he not realize that he was falling for her?

"Shit!" he screamed. He'd blown it. Just when she'd needed him the most, he'd screwed it up.

Chapter 15

Revitalize

Logan twitched, coated in a cold sweat. He hadn't been able to fall asleep for hours, with flashes of what could've been tormenting his exhausted mine. Trying to force his eyes closed failed him, and he stared into the darkness with only the taunting lights of the slow passage of time to accompany him.

"At least tomorrow's Saturday," he muttered to himself.

Getting up and heading toward the refrigerator, he grumbled the entire way, grabbing a protein shake and trying to ignore the absolute silence of the late Orrville night. Most of the victory parties had finally worn themselves out, but signs of life were welcome in a place where Logan feared death.

The landline phone suddenly rang, nearly making him jump through the ceiling. Who could possibly be calling him at this hour? He had his hopes, naturally.

"Logan?" a familiar female voice on the other line inquired.

"Yeah," Logan mumbled. "Who is this?"

"It's Erin."

Logan's stomach sank. He wasn't quite over the anger and regret she'd instilled in him by refusing to be there when he needed her the most. After so many years, how was it that easy to give up on everything for the sake of popularity and convenience?

"Hi," was all he said.

"So I'm sorry I called so late," she began, "but I needed to know if you were okay."

"What? Yeah, I'm fine," he lied. "Why do you ask?"

"I was there tonight."

"You were?"

"Of course. I'm on the cheerleading team, silly."

"Yeah," Logan dimly recalled. "Right."

"I saw what happened," she continued. "Are you hurt? Are you okay?" You don't sound like you are."

"I'm fine," he lied again.

"Can I come see you?"

"Why?"

That caught her a bit off-guard, but she tried not to let it affect her cause. "I feel bad about what happened. I want to talk about it. I mean, we've known each other so long. I don't want to lose you from my life completely, regardless of what happens, right?"

Sure, exactly, you demonstrated that the night you bailed on me, Logan screamed internally.

"Okay," was how the anger left his mouth.

"You want me to come over? Or do you wanna meet

somewhere?"

Logan considered this. "I know a place."

Even in the darkness, the rails shined, guiding the iron horses and illegal pedestrians alike along a pre-planned journey toward a different location. Logan had slipped on his old sneakers, and they could barely retain any grip against the moist metal road.

Finally, overlooking the bridge into the collector's yard, he sighed. All he could see at this hour were two old tank cars and a poorly marked crossing. It didn't feel right being here, but he couldn't quite figure out why. Something wasn't sitting right.

"This is a new one for you," Erin said, interrupting his internal dialogue. Meekly walking forward, her eyes gleamed off one of the few slivers of light escaping to this part of town. "Why here?"

Logan wasn't about to explain the significance of the location. Things were already complicated enough, and there was no need to further exacerbate the tearing feeling in the pit of his stomach.

"It's quiet," he said at last.

"It's quiet everywhere at this time of night," Erin pointed out. "Surely there's something more to it than that?"

"Nope," he fibbed. "Just felt like getting out."

"Why not the cemetery?" she asked.

He swallowed the pang of hurt. "Didn't want to be there right now. Too many bad memories."

"Never bothered you before."

"It does now," he snapped a little too harshly.

"Okay, sorry." Erin stepped back. "I didn't mean

anything by it." She kicked a rock against the iron guard rail. "I suppose it could grow on me."

"Yeah," he responded, not particularly interested in small-talk.

"I guess you're wondering why I wanted to talk," she said. "Why here? Why now, right?"

"I suppose."

"I feel bad, Logan," she explained. "I didn't mean for things to go down the way they did, but I didn't know what else to do."

"What do you mean?"

"You were so sad when your dad left, and I mean, I get it and all, but you were like, on another planet," she replied. "Nobody could get through to you, not even your friends. Not even me."

Logan shook his head, but Erin didn't notice. "It was rough," he offered as a defense.

"I know," she said softly, "and I should've been more understanding. It can't be easy not knowing if your father's going to come back home or not... Oh, god, I'm so sorry!"

Logan grimaced and turned away.

"Logan, stop!" she demanded.

"What else is there?" he asked her. "Twist the knife a little harder, why don't you?"

"I didn't mean it, Logan," she pleaded, "and I think you know that. I'm not trying to hurt you. I'm trying to understand."

"Understand what, Erin What else is there to possibly understand?"

"I guess... I guess I need to know why you felt the need to go hang out with her instead of everyone else."

"Who?"

"You know who."

Logan did know, but wanted to make her say it. "Who, Erin?"

"Ezra," she finally confirmed.

"Ellie," he corrected.

"Whatever."

"No, not whatever!" he yelled "You really don't get it at all, do you?"

"Get what?!"

"Get what it's like to be constantly referred to in the wrong way. Constantly told how you're supposed to feel, what you're supposed to say, how you're supposed to behave! It's bad enough that people don't think I should be allowed to have emotions when my father goes into a fucking warzone, but then the very same people have to misgender the only one who's been there for me the whole time!"

"Misgender?"

"You called her Ezra," Logan pointed out. "*Her* name is *Ellie.*"

"Are you in love with her, Logan?" Erin asked.

Logan didn't answer, staring off into the night instead. "Why did you come here, Erin? What's the point?"

Erin stood next to him, trying to discern what could be holding his interest, but failing to locate anything that stood out.

"I guess I had to know for sure," she offered.

"Know what?"

She turned toward him, grabbing his elbow to steady herself. "Whether or not I had made the right decision."

"And?"

"I didn't," she admitted. "It was probably the most heartless thing I could've done, and at the worst possible time."

Logan nodded, though he felt like he shouldn't have. It seemed rude to do at someone's apology.

"It's okay," he sputtered.

"No, it isn't," she said. "And if you don't ever forgive me, I totally get it." The tension relaxed a bit as they each took deep breaths; the exhales creating a small bit of visible vapor drifting upward. "I mean, I fucked up. What more can I say?"

"You don't need to say anything."

"Yeah I do, because I didn't before, and that was wrong."

"You made your choice," he said.

"What are you saying?"

"I'm saying that I cared about you for years, loved you with all my heart, but when things became inconvenient, when you could no longer just glide by on the status of being with me, you bailed."

"Logan, I…" Erin started to reply, but he held up his hand.

"Please, don't. I forgive you."

"You do?"

"Yes."

"So… We can try to fix this?" she asked.

Logan shook his head. "No."

Erin's face, aghast, became slightly illuminated from the tears forming in the corner of her eyes.

"No?" she repeated. "Why not?"

"I can't," he replied. "I mean, I'll never hold it against

you or anything, and I hold no bitterness or ill-will toward you at all."

"But?"

"But I need someone who is willing to be there for me all the time, and not just when it's convenient. And I'm sorry, Erin, but you weren't able to do that. Someone else was."

"Her?"

"It doesn't matter who."

"It *is* her," she stated flatly.

Logan against didn't answer, instead looking down at the ground and sliding his old shoe along a particularly shiny spot on the rails.

"Whatever it is," he answered with a sigh, "it wasn't what we had or what I needed. I'm sorry if I hurt you, but I can't lie to you and say that I'm willing to try again. I'm not."

"I respect that," Erin said, despite her visibly stricken state. "I suppose it's for the best."

"It will be," he said.

"But not yet."

"No, not yet."

She reached over and gave him a hug. It was much different than the ones she'd given him over the last eight years of their lives. It was a friendly hug, a caring hug, but clearly indicative of their new status.

"I hope he comes home," she whispered.

Logan hugged her back. "Me too."

Returning to bed shortly before dusk, Logan was amazed at how much easier it was to fall asleep that night, not to mention how much less interrupted it was. For the first time in what seemed like years, he felt like he could breathe without questioning it.

Eventually rising mid-Saturday afternoon, a small part of him secretly hoped the smell of frying eggs would greet his senses. Alas, it was not to be.

Pacing in the kitchen while he questioned everything he'd done recently, the world didn't exist outside of the inside of his head. For once, it was a safe place to be, and his gut wasn't trying to escape by any means necessary. It was all surprisingly peaceful.

He stepped out onto the wooden deck, overlooking the grassy hill of his yard. As a boy, he'd used that as the home run line, swinging away with all the power he had at his father's underhanded lobs.

"You'll grow up to play for the Tribe!" he recalled his father praising. "You'll grow up and forget all about your dad and football!"

"Never, Father," he whispered aloud. "I'd never forget you."

One particular memory replayed in front of him, as the third straight tennis ball went bouncing into the neighbor's yard. "Forget it," he laughed. "They're Michigan fans, they'll never return it!"

"Aw, come on," young Logan pleaded. "I'm a Buckeye, they'll never catch me!"

Robert shook his head, smiling at how much his son was already growing up like him. The two of them were particularly close, even at a young age, due to being mostly alone together.

"One day, son," he mused, "you're going to surprise even me."

"What do you mean, Father?" young Logan asked.

Robert knelt tenderly to his visibly sensitive boy, placing a comforting arm around him. His son was everything to him, and that was why he served his country as a career soldier. It was worth every second to care for the pride of his life.

"Son," he began as older Logan watched, "I may not be able to give you everything, but I'll give you all I have. That I can promise."

"Does that mean you're going to stay home from now on?" young Logan hoped.

"I wish I could," Robert replied with regret, "but that is how I make sure we're safe, Logan."

"Safe?" young Logan repeated, as if questioning the possibility of it being otherwise. "From what?"

Robert's gaze lengthened. "I don't know, son. But I do what I do to make sure it never gets to us. That's all I can do."

As his eyes remained on the horizon, a silhouette appeared in the sunset. "And it looks like someone else will always be looking out for you too."

Logan and young Logan both looked toward the sloping concrete driveway. Emerging was little Ezra, pre-change, pre-fallout, but so obviously feminine that Logan couldn't believe he never saw it before.

"Hi, Logan," young Ezra greeted the two. "Hello, sir!"

"Ezra Crow, for the last time, don't call me 'sir,' " Robert playfully instructed. "Call me 'Dad,' or 'second Dad,' if that's too awkward."

"Are you sure?" Ezra warily asked.

"I wouldn't say it if I wasn't, Ezra," Robert earnestly replied.

He rose to give Ezra a proper, firm handshake. Ezra shook his hand afterward, pretending it was painful. Robert then turned again to his son, squatting down to his eye-level, while present Logan watched on, barely containing himself.

"You see that, Logan?" Robert asked.

"What, Ezra?" young Logan replied.

Robert pointed toward the young Crow child. "This is your best friend. This is the one who loves you, more than any of your teammates, the girls, the boys, and everyone who will say they do. So many people will want something from you, and it'll seem so good at the time, but remember where your true love lies." Robert brought Ezra in with a side-hug, pointing toward both himself and the young boy. "Here, and here."

Young Logan pointed toward his own heart in return. "And here," he added.

"And there," Robert agreed.

"Now, let's play!" young Logan demanded.

His father chuckled. "You got it."

"Come on." Logan motioned toward Ezra. "You play outfield!"

"That's okay," Ezra said. "I'll watch."

"Suit yourself!" Logan picked up his aluminum bat. "Let's go, Dad!"

"Watch this one, it's got a curve," Robert teased as he tossed one in. *Smack!* This one sailed well over the hill in the air. Logan raised his arm in celebration.

"You'll be outslugging Albert Belle in no time," Robert laughed.

Young Logan smiled in appreciation. What Logan didn't notice before, however, was young Ezra standing right there. Right near him. Eyes never leaving him. Never leaving his side. Watching out for him, the way he always had.

Present Logan relived the memory with emotions he'd never felt before. Noticing these things sent his sense of self, his sense of his history, into a tailspin. Perhaps nothing was as he thought it was. Perhaps what was true back then, he was too stupid and blind to see.

Young Logan playfully rubbed little Ezra's shoulder, and Ezra smiled in return. When young Logan looked away, there grew a blush in Ezra's cheeks. Those feminine cheeks, that swaying saunter...

My god, thought Logan. *That really is how she's always been. And she's always been around, always been watching, always been...*

Here.

Logan wiped both of his eyes with the back of his wrist. He scanned the reaches of his backyard as the projections dissipated. His head dropped in disappointment as the realization washed over him more by the second.

He closed the screen door behind him, with one last hopeful glance into the yard. Nothing. Maybe he'd finally screwed up enough that she'd gone away for good. Logan hoped not, but had learned to live with his guilt and regret.

The lights shut off inside the house. Finally, some leaves rustled nearby, and Ellie moved from her hiding spot near the garage door at the bottom of the hill. Her eyes were nearly as drowned with tears as Logan's were. She'd always be there, even when he didn't know it. That was all she knew how to do, and all she ever wanted.

"Someday," she hoped out loud before disappearing back into the night. "Someday."

Chapter 16

Decision

Monday morning, Logan arose on time. Not even looking at his clock, he turned off the alarm, grabbed his Monday practice gear, and sat down in the kitchen. The vegetables and bread were exactly where he'd left them, and he'd checked out a book Ellie had recommended.

Walking to a school was a nice change for him. He didn't have to dodge any traffic, have his nerves shoot up for being late, or worry about facing further minor infractions from the school. He didn't quite know how to process being this relaxed in the mornings, but it was nice.

He strolled into the front door well before anyone else noticed him, and was immediately showered in the color of all the Orrville Red Rider streamers and decorations. Divisions were Friday against Wooster, and it at least made everyone forget about the ugliness that had gone on… he hoped, anyway.

Kathy and Alice approached him, and Logan was ready to verbally defend himself until he saw them signaling they came in peace.

"Hey, Logan," Kathy said.

"Hi," Alice added.

"Hi," Logan replied. "What can I do for you?"

"Well…" Kathy started.

"We just wanted to say…" Alice continued.

"Yes?"

"We have her back," Alice finally stammered out.

"Her back?" Logan questioned.

"Ellie's," Kathy confirmed. "We're watching out for her."

Logan raised his eyebrows. "What do you mean?"

"It's rivalry week," Kathy replied, "and that protestor guy's been all over the news yelling about her."

"Yeah," Alice continued, "he's lobbying for the school to pass a rule about who can use the bathroom."

"Use the bathroom?" Logan quizzically responded. "Why?"

"They know about her," Kathy explained.

"What about her?"

"That she's…"

"Different," Alice supplied.

Kathy nodded. "Yeah."

Logan's temperature began to rise. So much for relaxation. "What'd he say?"

"He called for visual inspection of any student who might be using the 'wrong' bathroom," answered Alice.

"I see," he growled. "And who the fuck would be doing the inspecting? Him?"

"I don't know," Alice replied.

He threw up his hands. "How is it any of his business, anyway?!"

Kathy shook her head. "I don't know."

"Where is he?" Logan's eyes darted around the hallway.

Alice cocked her head. "Who?"

"Pastor Carl," Logan said, "or whatever his name is."

"He was on the news this morning," Kathy answered.

"Channel 3," Alice added.

Without another word, Logan took off for the front door. Mr. Briner saw him on a mission and tried to stop him.

"Where do you think you're going, sir?"

"Get out of my way," Logan demanded.

"Logan," Mr. Briner warned, "I know what this is about. Don't do it. That's what he wants from you."

"And what I want from you," Logan muttered, "is to get out of my way. Right now."

"I saw nothing." Mr. Briner grinned a bit despite himself. He stepped out of Logan's way and let him crash through the front door.

Outside, Ellie was just arriving at school and saw Logan making off in haste. She started backing up and trying to keep pace with him, but failed.

"What are you doing…? Hey, come back!"

But Logan had no intention of stopping. "I've got this, Ellie."

"Don't do it!" she screamed. "It's not worth it!"

"Go ahead to school. I will take care of this."

"You know better than that," she shouted back. "I'm still pissed at you, but I'm coming with you!"

The two nearly ran into Erin, who was coming around the corner on the sidewalk from the opposite direction. Logan broke stride only for a minute to avoid her, but Ellie wasn't as used to dodging people in her path, and they collided.

Logan, looking back, stopped and turned around to help them up. "What's going on?" Erin asked, brushing dirt off her outfit.

"Can you make sure she's okay?" Logan inquired.

Erin's expression was one of instant understanding, and she nodded. Logan turned back and darted off before Ellie could fully regain her composure. She tried to follow him, but Erin grabbed her arm.

"Get the fuck off me!" Ellie screamed.

"Let him go, Ell," Erin pleaded.

"Why?"

"He knows what he's doing," Erin explained. "When he gets like this, just let him do what he needs to. Come on." She motioned toward the school. "I'll help you."

"Help me with what?"

"I don't know," Erin replied, "but I feel like I should."

At the Channel 3 building in downtown Orrville, Pastor Carl and his supporters placarded several surrounding businesses. Next to Pastor Carl, there was a poster of a girl who had a red X through her dress, and the text read: *No Men in Women's Bathrooms.*

As Logan steamed closer, he realized the girl in the picture was Ellie.

Pastor Carl had his megaphone and was blasting his verbal harassment at anyone passing by, whether they paid attention or not. "Are we going to continue to let our wives and daughters be subjected to men in dresses?"

"No!" one of the protestors replied.

"Amen!" shouted another.

"Are we..." Pastor Carl stopped when he saw Logan approaching with a purpose. "Well, look what we have here, everyone!" he announced, diverting the crowd's attention. "The fag-lover himself!"

Logan parted the crowd with his sheer presence and came face-to-face with his nemesis. "Take it down," he growled.

"Take what down?" Pastor Carl snidely answered. "The picture of your boyfriend in a dress there? Why? We don't want that boy in the bathroom with our daughters!"

"Take... it... down," Logan repeated through his teeth. "And *her* name is *fucking* Ellie, you self-righteous hypocrite!"

"Ooh." Pastor Carl feigned shock. "The jock learned some big words, did he? Your boyfriend teach you those? That'll help. You'll need good conversation when you're burning in Hell, sinner!"

That was it. Logan snapped.

Pastor Carl ducked like he was going to get hit, but Logan reached for the poster, not the pastor, and he ripped it in half. He took the half he had in his hand and threw it aside, then grabbed the other and crumpled it into a ball. Seeing that Pastor Carl dropped his megaphone when he ducked, he snatched it up.

"Give that back," the pastor demanded, but Logan was easily able to hold him at bay with his other arm.

"Is this what this town has come to?" Logan asked. "All the problems we have in the world, and you're worried about where Ellie goes to the bathroom?"

"We don't want our daughters to get molested!" someone yelled back.

"Name one time when Ellie has been accused of molestation," Logan replied. "Or given any indication that she behaves in such a way. Anyone?"

Amongst the crowd, a Channel 3 cameraman was filming Logan as he spoke. Seeing the star Red Rider conducting an address, more onlookers began to gather.

Back in Mrs. Mazaj's class, Jamie came running through the door, interrupting the lecture.

"Turn on the TV!" she commanded.

"Jamie, you're late, and you interrupted the lesson!"

"Logan's on TV!" she exclaimed.

Ellie's heart soared. Erin gently rubbed her shoulder.

Curiosity piqued, Mrs. Mazaj turned on the television as requested. Logan appeared on the screen.

"I've lived in this town my whole life," he was saying. "We've always been a community. My father proudly served his country, seeking revenge on those who harmed us."

"Your father's a great man," someone in the crowd added.

"But he's not over there fighting so that fags can dress up and use the girl's bathroom!" Pastor Carl yelled as loudly as he could. "If I knew I could change the rules just by saying I felt like a girl one day, I'd have gotten into the girl's locker room myself!"

A smirk graced Logan's face. "So you're telling me that you would've gone in the girl's locker room, and the only thing stopping you was not being a girl?"

"That's the way God intended," Pastor Carl argued.

"I think it's far more likely that someone interested in sneaking into the girl's locker room is going to molest someone than someone just trying to go about their day and be left alone," Logan proclaimed.

"It's the same thing!"

"No!" Logan shouted him down, making him back away. "It isn't! Ellie is a girl. She has always been a girl, and deserves to be called what she asked to be called."

"It's not what's on her birth certificate!"

"How is that any of your fucking business?" Logan demanded. "It isn't. None of it is. You don't even have a kid in this school! You're just trying to get everyone riled up about something you don't understand to drive up church attendance, and you're using Ellie's reference—illegally, I might add—to make your bigoted, narrow-minded point."

"Yeah!" a different voice in the crowd agreed.

"Let him speak!" another chimed in.

"Ellie is the most genuine person I've ever met, and she deserves the same respect that you'd give me or anyone else. You should be ashamed, any of you who were using her image to scare people. You wouldn't have done this to any of the other girls at Orrville High, and her being different does not give you the license to make her the logo of your smear campaign!"

Logan stepped over to another sign and tore it in half. "Let it be known that if I see any more of these, especially if they have Ellie's picture on them, I will boycott the division game against Wooster."

A huge cry of surprise arose from both the crowd on TV and the one in the classroom.

"You can't do that!" Pastor Carl howled.

Logan turned around to him once again, standing inches from his face. "Try me." He pushed the megaphone back into the pastor's hands. Then he stepped away, but before he left, he grabbed a placard on a stick and broke it over his knee, dropping it on each side of him as he left.

Cheers sprang up from the crowd, and Ellie blushed as she cried into her hands. When she moved them to see, nearly everyone in the class was looking at her and smiling.

In one of the freshman rooms, Josh stood proudly. "That goes for me too!" he announced.

In his own classroom, Coach Stewert nodded in agreement. "None of us will play if Logan doesn't."

Bernie and Jimmy stared at each other with disdain, shaking their heads.

Ellie rose from her chair and started walking to the door.

"Where are you going?" Mrs. Mazaj asked.

She didn't respond, instead opening the door and walking out, both smiling and in tears. Other students started followed her down the hall, each instinctively knowing what was going on.

Mrs. Mazaj threw up her hands. "Hell with it," she laughed, and followed the rest of her students.

Outside, Ellie descended the school steps with several dozen students watching her from inside. Logan came running around the corner, then stopped as he saw Ellie standing there, red-faced. The two stared at each other for several seconds, a million words being exchanged between then with none spoken at all.

First Logan moved toward her, then Ellie toward him.

She leapt into his arms and Logan held her tightly, spinning her around as cheers erupted from the student body huddled at the entrance of the school. The two of them were completely oblivious to anyone else noticing what was going on at all.

Finally, Logan stopped spinning and set her back on her feet.

Ellie barely managed to whisper, "You idiot!"

"I won't let anyone hurt you ever again," Logan promised. "I love you, Ellie."

Ellie gently grabbed both his cheeks, and they kissed for the first time, losing themselves in each other and the moment. They stopped long enough for her to respond, "I love you, Logan. I always have."

"I know," he replied. "Me too."

Chapter 17

Wrong

Logan and Ellie held hands through the hallway, many supportive glances, hugs, and hand waves following them everywhere they went. It seemed like a different school from the one that had told Logan how wrong he was to have feelings only weeks ago.

Logan snuck many glances at Ellie's beaming face. He'd never seen her so happy. She wore that sarcastic head-tilt like a badge of honor, but for once there was no irony in her face, no sardonic nature to her words.

"It's strange," she mused.

"What's strange?"

"This. All of this."

"What about it?"

"I've watched you for years, walking down the hall, completely oblivious to the awe in everyone's eyes as they see you," she explained. "I was always one of those people, but for a different reason."

"What reason was that?"

Ellie squeezed his hand a little tighter. "Even during our years of silence, I saw the person you were, and the one you would become."

Logan considered this, nodding. "Like that day, with Josh?"

"You remember that?"

"How could I forget?"

"Until recently, I thought you'd forgotten about everything," Ellie admitted.

Logan laughed a little, mostly in reference to how his memory truly worked. "I remember some things that didn't happen, but I rarely forget something that did. Sometimes I have a hard time telling the two apart, but I haven't forgotten anything that involved you."

"Not even the bad stuff?"

"Not even the bad stuff."

Ellie leaned her head on his shoulder. He pulled her closer, and they moved as one. "This is nice," she hummed.

"It is," he agreed.

"So... you were saying?"

"Right," Logan continued. "It was Wooster week... the first one, obviously, not this one... and there was this helpless-looking kid. I remember feeling that helpless."

"Oh, bullshit." Ellie smacked him playfully. "Like anyone messed with Coach Ramsay's son!"

"Not in public..." He trailed off, then shook his head as if trying to dismiss a bad vibe. "But before I could break from the morning daily routine, and help quell the dragons that are Bernie and Jimmy, you were there."

"I was."

"You were so… fearless," he said. "That's what I loved about the way you handled it. You helped that kid with no fear whatsoever. You didn't worry that Bernie and Jimmy were on the team, or how much bigger than you they were, just… bam, verbal missiles right to the brain."

"Freshmen have enough to worry about without appeasing guys who get their rocks off by hurting others."

"But it's not something you *had* to do," Logan explained. "You did it because it was the right thing. That's what you've always done."

Ellie modestly looked away. "I've tried."

"I wish I could have that same drive," Logan responded.

She snapped her head back and tilted it in confusion. "What do you mean?"

"I see you," he said. "I see all that you do. School, the newspaper, standing up for people… I admire you so much."

"Well, thank you, and I do appreciate that, but I meant why do you think you don't have that same drive?"

"I'm not able to do half the things you do, Ell."

Ellie stopped, bringing both of them to face each other. "I've seen you overcome difficulties that most people don't know exist." She cradled his chin in her hands. "I've seen what it's done to you, and how others treated your episodes like they were invisible… like *you* were invisible."

Logan gently rubbed her right hand, taking in every word she said.

"And," she added, "not once have I seen you blame someone else for what's happened. Not once have I seen you take your frustrations out on someone weak, or blame your father's absence for your shortcomings. You try to take on the world every single day, but your biggest enemy is what's inside your own head. Having to overcome the monsters in there has to be the scariest thing in the world."

"I feel bad," he muttered.

"Why?"

"Because I feel so selfish," he sighed. "Like, nobody knows where Father is, and he might be dead, and all I've been able to think about is my own stupid problems."

"They're not stupid, Logan," Ellie countered.

"But what about that night, in the cemetery?"

"Oh..." Ellie blushed, "when I threw my tits at you?"

"That's one way of putting it."

Ellie kissed him on the cheek. "We all have our moments of weakness," she explained. "That was one of mine."

"But what was it about, anyway?"

"You really wanna know?" she asked.

"Yes," he assured her.

"Some of your buddies were misgendering me that night."

"Yeah?"

"Yeah," Ellie echoed, "and it got to me. It usually doesn't, but that night, it did."

"Why do you think that is?" he asked her.

"I was vulnerable."

"Why?"

"You," she giggled. "Seeing you do that, watching the moment unfold live before my eyes... I was so proud of you, but all things have their consequence."

"So the consequence of being happy about

something that happened was that you couldn't defend yourself, and then you got mad at me?"

"Logan," Ellie replied, "I know it's been awhile since I started transitioning, but these hormones are still relatively new. Imagine going through puberty all over again, and that's what it's like."

"Really?"

"Yeah."

"So, when does your voice start cracking?" he joked.

"You asshole," she played back.

"Like, does it crack *up* this time? Is that how it works?"

"Stop it!" she laughed again.

"Or is it that upward inflection? Is that what they call it? Where everything sounds like a question?" he teased.

"What the hell am I gonna do with you?" she sighed.

"Keep me around, I hope," he answered, breaking the breezy dialogue between them with a moment of honesty. It caught her off guard. "Weren't expecting that, were ya?"

"Sometimes what you hope most for, you think will never come," she retorted. "I never expected to hear words like that from you, ever."

"I didn't expect to fall in love with you, my best friend. More than that, now."

"You've always been more than that to me."

Logan leaned down and kissed Ellie on the lips. "As you are to me."

"Promise?"

"Promise."

The bell rung, interrupting their joyful moment. "I gotta go. Newspaper."

"See you tonight?"

"Of course."

They snuck one more kiss in before the crowd in the hall washed them away like the tide. Everyone was in a hurry to get somewhere. Everyone except Bernie and Jimmy, anyway, who stood down the hall from Logan like two guardsmen at the castle wall.

Approaching cautiously, Logan waved at them with a forced smile. "Hey guys."

The two didn't return the greeting. "You know what I think?" Jimmy asked Bernie.

"That Patty Mayonnaise was kinda hot?"

"Not that," Jimmy replied. "Okay, besides that…"

"Better."

"I think that Logan here has his head out of the game," Jimmy snarled. "Might take someone to remind him where it needs to go."

"I think you're right," Bernie agreed.

"Guys," Logan helplessly countered, "my head's in the game. I'll be there."

"Oh, I'm sure you will," Jimmy replied.

"But that's not where your mind will be," Bernie added.

"What the hell do you mean by that?" Logan demanded.

"We think your little boyfriend is too much of a distraction, Logan," Bernie said

"Girlfriend," Logan corrected. "She's my girlfriend. Get it right."

Wham! Jimmy's fist slammed into the pit of Logan's stomach, knocking the air from his lungs. Before he could inhale, a knee smacked up against his forehead, sending him sprawling to the ground.

"The problem is," Bernie growled while Jimmy opened a classroom door, "I don't give a shit what you want to call that fucking drag queen—you're not the player we need right now." He took off his jacket and kicked Logan in the ribs. "Coast is clear."

Jimmy grabbed the lapel of Logan's jacket, tearing it as he pulled Logan up. Logan kicked him away, but Bernie had him behind the arms.

"That was stupid," Jimmy pointed out, and he sucker-punched Logan again in the gut, then crushed his jaw with a blow that made blood spew from his mouth. His lips swelled, bleeding everywhere, and Bernie tossed him inside the classroom. The two followed him in, shutting the door behind them.

"So we," Jimmy continued, "decided to teach you a little lesson." He landed another kick in Logan's ribs. "Because you have turned into some kind of sick freak, and nobody wants that leading their football team."

"Nobody," Bernie agreed before turning a desk over onto Logan. "We'll be the laughingstock of the whole fucking state, Logan. 'Oh, did you guys hear about those Red Riders?' 'You mean the ones with the faggot running back who likes pretty boys?' You see the problem here?"

Logan spat more blood onto the gray carpet. "She's a girl," he wheezed.

Bernie laughed, then threw the desk off him and pulled him up to his face by the collar. "You just don't learn, do you?"

"That's your fucking problem," added Jimmy, kicking him in the spine while Bernie held him up.

"So don't make us repeat this lesson, or you're not

even going to make it to states," Bernie warned. "And if you show up with that flamer, we'll take both of you and do much, much worse."

"Don't you fucking touch her," Logan snapped, then spit in Bernie's face, dousing his cheek with blood and saliva. He struggled, but wasn't putting up much of a fight at this point. Not one that would affect anything, at least.

Bernie nodded, letting the blood drip down the side of his cheek, then punched Logan across the jaw once more. Logan landed flat on his back, coughed, and curled up into a ball.

"There's our star," Jimmy taunted. "Our star running back, bleeding on the floor. Where's your boyfriend to rescue you?"

"Nowhere," Bernie continued. "At least, not yet."

"No," Logan choked out.

"Don't worry, we'll take good care of him," Jimmy assured.

"Stop," Logan croaked.

"You're in no position to demand anything!" Bernie screamed. "Now get your fucking head straight before Wooster, or we'll set both of you queers straight ourselves."

Bernie and Jimmy walked out, the door slamming behind them. The lights in the room turned off as Logan writhed in pain.

"Ellie," he managed to whisper before falling unconscious.

Chapter 18

Complications

"I need help in here!"

Footsteps echoed down the hallway, and Josh lifted Logan's head off the floor, cradling it in his arms. "Logan, are you okay? Can you hear me?"

Logan's eyes, glazed and red, peeked through his lids. "Josh? What...?"

"Logan, who did this?" Josh demanded.

"Where's Ellie?" Logan asked, trying to get up.

"You're not going anywhere. You're in rough shape." Josh turned his head toward the door. "I said, I need some goddamned help in here!"

Mr. Solemekin came bursting through the door with several other of their teammates in tow. "My god," Mr. Solemekin muttered. "What happened?"

Two of Logan's teammates rushed over while Josh gently held his head. They lifted him to his feet, but Logan fell back into one of them.

"Someone kicked the shit out of him," one of them observed.

"No shit, Sherlock," Josh snapped. "Who did this, Logan?"

"Ellie," Logan repeated. "Help Ellie."

"Help Ellie? Did someone hurt him too?"

"Her," Logan corrected, even in his delirious state.

"Her—sorry," Josh said. "Did someone hurt her too?"

"I don't know," Logan responded, trying to shove away his teammates. "Let me go, I have to help her!"

"Who did this?" Mr. Solemekin asked in a stern tone. "Was it one of your teammates?"

Logan ignored his request too, finally coming to stand on his own without them grabbing him. He tried to shove past Mr. Solemekin, but he wasn't having any of it.

"Hey, Ramsay!" he called, holding him back. "Tell me who did this, and I'll have their asses charged with assault."

Logan stared at the ground, then brought his eyes to Mr. Solemekin's. "This is what you wanted, isn't it?"

"What the Hell do you mean by that?"

"That little talk we had," Logan said. "The betterment of the team, embarrassing everyone, weird, uncomfortable... all those things?"

"I didn't... want anyone to get hurt," stammered Mr. Solemekin.

"And you thought the best way to do that was by hurting people, as long as they're queer or different?" Logan accused.

"I will not have my judgment questioned by a child,"

Mr. Solemekin fired back. "Now tell me, who did this?"

"Find out yourself." Logan grimaced, holding his jaw. "You can tell the cops that they were just celebrating the old American pastime of beating up faggots."

"That's not fair at all," Mr. Solemekin called at Logan as he limped toward the doorway. "You stop right there, young man!"

Logan halted, standing in the doorway, but not looking back.

"Tell me what happened here," Mr. Solemekin pressed once more.

"Boys being boys," Logan responded. He then slammed the door shut behind him.

Mr. Solemekin adjusted his blazer with a huff. He turned toward the three football players, who were staring daggers at him. "What are you looking at? You guys were in on this too."

"You told him that?" Josh asked. "You told him that you wanted this?"

"No," Mr. Solemekin denied. "I told him what was right for the school, and the team."

"Yeah," Josh sneered, "and how'd that turn out?"

"Josh," one of the two other players butted in. "Coach Stewert did tell us to leave him there that one day."

"And tell me when he said, 'And if he really loves the girl, beat the shit out of him.' When was that, Einstein??" Josh yelled.

"Enough," Mr. Solemekin interrupted. "I'll not have my reputation spoken of in such ways."

"Go fuck yourself!" Josh shouted back.

"Excuse me?"

"You heard me."

"You're suspended, son," Mr. Solemekin growled. "I'll not tolerate that kind of language, especially when it's directed at the vice principal."

"Well, it's there, so I don't know what you're going to do about it," Josh muttered. He motioned toward the door, and the two teammates followed.

"Where are you going?" Mr. Solemekin asked.

"To find the guys," Josh replied.

"Why?"

"We may not agree with everyone," Josh answered, "but when one of our teammates is in danger, we protect our brother."

The two teammates left in front of Josh, before he stared daggers through his vice principal. "No matter who he loves."

Running shoes battled the concrete the whole way down the dampened streets. The sun turned orange on the horizon, and Logan gasped for every breath as he moved as fast as he could. A car honked as it nearly flattened him on the street, sliding past him. Logan sputtered up to the sidewalk, but collapsed on the curb.

"Logan? What happened to you? Are you all right?"

"Erin!"

Erin ran over just as the rain began to fall. She pulled him to his feet.

"Bernie… Jimmy," Logan gasped.

"What about them?"

"They attacked me," Logan replied, "and they're going after Ellie."

"Get in," she instructed.

"Why?"

"Just do it!" she insisted, motioning toward the car. Logan conceded, getting into the passenger's side.

"Where do you think she would go?" Erin asked once she started the car.

"Only one place I can think of."

Logan slipped in the grass, landing in a spat of mud near a thick tree. "Come on," Erin encouraged him while trying to pick him up. "You can do it! She needs you!"

Logan's legs powered him through a crawl to the break in the woods where the track ran. "Is this it?" Erin inquired.

"Yes, down this way," Logan yelled over the sound of the pouring rain. "Careful of the rocks!"

Rocks kicked everywhere by each footstep, the rails glimmering in their soaked state. A lightning bolt pierced the night sky, followed by a shockingly loud thunder clap. Logan covered his head and ears, screaming in reaction.

"Logan!" Erin screamed. "Logan! Come on, focus!"

"The loud!"

"I know, but we have to keep going!"

Logan grimaced, removing his arms from his head, his hair matted to his forehead from the rain. "It's not much farther!"

Taking off again, Logan and Erin sprinted as fast as they could through the monsoon-like conditions, trying not to trip over the rocks that held up the rails.

"Over there!" Logan finally pointed out ahead of their path.

"The bridge?"

"Yes!"

As they put their heads down, running full speed ahead, a dark figure popped in front of them just before they hit the bridge area. Logan slid into a stop, Erin rushing up behind him.

"You should've stayed home," a voice accused. "It would've been better for you."

"Bernie, what the fuck are you doing?" Erin yelled.

"Doing what needs to be done," Jimmy responded from several yards away. Logan's eyes darted past the mountain of meat that Bernie was.

"Don't even think about it, or she'll get it worse," Bernie warned.

Logan saw Ellie, nearly unconscious, being held up by her hair in Jimmy's fist. Her top was torn and her skirt was gone. Her eyes pleaded for help.

"What kind of monster are you?!" Logan shouted.

"Not as bad as the ones you faggots are gonna find in Hell!"

"Logan!" Ellie cried. Jimmy yanked on her ponytail, and Logan could see what they'd done, and what they were planning on continuing to do.

"What, you got something to say?"

"Nope."

"What?"

Logan speared Bernie to the ground, causing them both to roll off the tracks from the momentum. Erin sprinted toward Jimmy, who held the half-naked and terrified Ellie in front of her.

"What is this?" Jimmy asked. "Old girl saves the new boy?"

"It looks like assault to me," Erin accused.

Logan broke free from Bernie, but Bernie grabbed

his leg and threw him to the ground. Jimmy released his grip on Ellie and opened both arms in front of Erin, inviting her to try to do something about it.

A train horn sounded in the distance. Bernie ran toward the track, but Logan tackled him from behind. Jimmy turned to see if the train signal was coming from these tracks, and Erin kicked him in the crotch.

"You fucking bitch!" he howled. "You're next!"

Jimmy hobbled toward Erin as Logan and Bernie continued trading punches and slipping in the mud. Jimmy grabbed for Erin, getting ahold of her jacket and pulling her back toward the track.

"You should've stayed away," he snarled.

A faint light started illuminating the woods. The low rumble of a diesel came closer, and the horn sounded again. Bernie slipped out of Logan's chokehold. Erin pulled free from her jacket and sprang away from Jimmy. Bernie grabbed her before she could get away, and Logan tripped Jimmy on the tracks.

The train hurtled toward them, the source of the light now visible.

"Bernie!" Jimmy screamed, realizing what was coming. Bernie turned to look, and Erin clocked him in the eye.

Bernie stumbled back, holding his hand over his face. "All this over some guy?"

Bernie suddenly burst forward like a cobra striking, then smacked to the ground with force. The train's rumble became deafening as it neared the bridge. It sounded another whistle, warning that it couldn't stop.

Logan, seeing Bernie on the ground, grabbed Jimmy by the back of his jacket and threw him off the tracks seconds before the diesel engine roared by, separating the two parties. Logan tried to look between the cars, but couldn't see much as the train went through.

Jimmy started to stir, but Logan held a boot on the back of his neck. "Don't even fucking think about it, Jimmy."

"Logan," Jimmy protested. "I'm your teammate!"

"You're nothing," Logan snapped. "Nothing."

When the train passed, Bernie remained on the ground. Ellie, heaving and hysterical, kicked him several more times before Erin finally pulled her away.

As the two struggled, Bernie pulled out a switchblade. Erin turned around to protect Ellie, and when Logan tried to run over, Jimmy wouldn't let go of his leg.

"Bernard!" a new voice broke through the night.

Bernie looked around, questioning the source. "Who called me that?"

Josh stepped through the trees. "Put the knife down," he commanded.

"Aren't we just having ourselves a queer little party here?" Bernie taunted.

More Orrville football players stepped around Josh. Bernie, Logan, and Jimmy stopped and turned to see their teammates surrounding them in every direction. The distraction allowed Logan to break free of Jimmy's grasp and run to Ellie. He wrapped his coat around her and hugged her tight.

"It's all over now," he whispered. "It's all over."

Coach Stewert stepped forward with two Orrville police officers. "That's them, officers. Bernard, James…"

"You're under arrest," one of the officers declared.

The two looked helplessly at Erin, Logan, and Ellie.

Logan glared back at the two of them as the officers cuffed them both.

Once they were secure, other teammates ran to their star running back, his girlfriend, and the heroic Erin, offering jackets to warm them up and shield them from the rain.

Bernie and Jimmy were escorted away from the scene, down the hill toward the road where a police cruiser awaited. Coach Stewert approached the trio, being tended to as gently as high school football players could.

"It's all over. You're safe now," he said.

Ellie buried her face into Logan's shoulder, tears streaming from her eyes as heavy as the rain. All he could do was hug her tighter, no matter how wracked with pain his body was.

The team led an escort for all three of them down the bridge, where they could see Bernie and Jimmy being loaded into the car.

"I'm sorry," Logan whispered into Ellie's ear. "I'm so sorry."

Chapter 19

Letter

Dear Father,

I don't know if you can, or ever will be able to, read you what I'm writing right now. The world has changed so much, and I've been given no update as to your status. All I know is that you're missing, and the world is not right without you here, and I'm having a hard time with that.

So many things have happened since you left. We're in the playoffs, Erin and I broke up, I've started speaking out, but most of all, I'm in love with my best friend. Somehow I doubt that'll surprise you, because you always seemed to know everything else before I told you, but I didn't know, so I needed to tell you now.

I know you may have once considered him to be "Ezra," and to be honest, it was difficult for me at first, even when we met again and she saved my life. But I get it now; she's always been a girl, and she's always been in love with me. It doesn't matter what her gender is. I'm in love with her. She's the only one in this world outside of you that understands me on the deepest of levels.

There were times when I doubted it, or worried so much about what other people would think that I became short-sighted. I'm sorry if I've ever let you down the same way, but know that I'm trying, learning, and growing from this experience. Having a brilliant best friend and girl to help me along the way has helped to streamline the process.

The big game is coming up against Wooster, and it's still not the same without Coach Ramsay on the sideline. Needless to say, your cool but intimidating demeanor and presence are highly missed, even by the coaches. They all eventually came around; all except for Jimmy and Bernie, but hopefully justice will prevail on those accounts. I guess I never really considered what friendship and love were until I was forced to see what losing it can cause.

We've fought, argued, left in a huff, been confused, apologized, stood up for each other, but we've never broken. Jimmy and Bernie tried to break us, and while the physical and mental scars may take a long time to heal, going through it together is what made it so strong in the first place. Our bond is truly like no other.

Father, I hope this letter finds you in good spirits, whatever that may mean or entail. I miss you every single day, and I hope you're home safe by the time this is all over. No matter how in love I am, my life will never be complete with you missing like this.

I've come to the realization that regardless of what

transpires with finding you, you'll never coach me again. I'm pretty sure Coach at Ohio State isn't going to be accepting or needing any new assistants anytime soon, as they're undefeated and heading toward that national championship we've all clamored for. I'm going to bring Orrville the State Championship as well, and when I become a Buckeye, it'll be because of you and Ellie that I was able to get there and become the person I am.

I never learned a lot of the lessons you wanted me to, but the ones that stuck with me came to my aid in the most vital and desperate of times. When I was being assaulted, it was one thing; I take beatings every day, but when I saw what they did to Ellie, I knew what the right thing to do was. Nobody should ever have to suffer through such horror, and I hate myself only for not getting to her sooner. I hope she doesn't hate me too… I don't know what I'd do without her.

Pastor Carl will continue to preach against us, making himself the victim in the big, mean football player pointing out that his hate speech is hate speech. I'll be there to keep fighting, and hopefully someone will stand in my stead once Ellie and I are off to Columbus.

Oh, there's no way in Hell I'm leaving without her. She got into Ohio State with an academic scholarship, so we've already both got "ins." The future is bright for us, or at least it will be when we finally get through this terrible episode. I've been waiting for the doctors to come out and tell me something, anything about her condition. She's the strongest person I know, so she'll make it through, but still, this wait is agonizing.

Be well, Father. I miss you. I love you. Please come home safe, or at least be alive. The world needs more of you and less of Pastor Carl.

Your son,

Logan Ramsay

Chapter 20

Truth

"And that's all you have to say, son?"

Logan stood in front of the police officers with disbelief in his eyes. "Why do I even need to say more?"

"Well," the taller one responded, "things aren't that simple."

"Seems pretty simple to me," Logan snarled.

"Son," the other officer replied, "this case will never get anywhere, not under these circumstances."

"And just what circumstances do you mean?"

The officers exchanged uncomfortable glances before the tall one put a hand on his shoulder. "I know you care about him a lot…"

"Her," Logan adamantly corrected.

"The law doesn't see it that way at the current time. I mean no disrespect. The point is, it's all hearsay at this point. There's nothing to indicate that Ezra didn't have interest or provoke them into these actions."

"Provoke them?!" Logan screamed. "Are you fucking kidding me? They assaulted both of us!"

"According to the boys," the shorter officer began, "Ezra was so convinced that he was female that he dressed up every day and provoked those boys into an advance that he decided later he didn't want. The boys were so shocked to find out that he was a drag queen that their reaction was appropriately shocked."

"So that means the reaction should be to beat the shit out of both of us?" Logan sneered.

"Son," the taller officer again began.

"Get your hand off me," Logan demanded.

"Whoa," the short officer declared, "we mean you no disrespect."

"No, you're just saying that it's her fault for existing in a space with a couple of sociopaths who assaulted me, and probably did worse to her."

"Again," the tall officer repeated, "the law doesn't see it that way. It's a legal defense to say that your friend there provoked them into these actions by tricking them into thinking that he was female."

"*She*, goddammit!" Logan muttered. "And she *is* female."

"Not according to his birth certificate," the shorter officer explained. "And that's all we really have to go on."

"It doesn't matter what he says," the tall officer continued. "According to the other two, Ezra convinced himself that he was a girl and then teased the boys into action. He tricked them, and they responded appropriately. They said they might even consider pressing harassment charges for Ezra trying to tempt those good boys into a dangerous situation, especially with lying about who he was to do it."

"So, that's it?" Logan shook his head. "Because you don't get it, because they made some shit up to get out of trouble, you're just letting them go? After what they did to her? Me? With all these witnesses?"

"We have no grounds to give you legal advice," the shorter officer retorted.

"If you want to pursue any further action, I'd contact an attorney," the tall officer suggested. "There's nothing more we can do."

Logan watched the two officers disappear into the elevator, and it was all he had inside him to not scream for the heavens. Erin, Kathy, Alice, Jamie, Josh, and several other teammates stood by in the waiting room, watching Logan's emotions get the better of him in so many ways.

Josh started to get up to try to help, but Erin held his wrist. "What are you doing?" he asked.

"Let him go," Erin instructed.

"Why? He's upset!"

"Yes," Erin replied, "he is. And he needs to be. But it's our job to be there for him, not make it about ourselves."

"But…"

"Sit down, Josh," Kathy demanded. "He'll let us know when we're needed.

"Physically, the worst that happened was a few tears."

Logan winced at the thought, but dared to ask for details anyway. "What kind of tears?"

"You don't want to know, son," the doctor claimed.

"And I'm sure your friend will tell you if she wants to."

Logan smiled a bit. "Thank you for addressing her correctly."

"I'm a medical professional," the doctor replied. "It's not my place to judge, nor force my beliefs on anyone for any reason."

"Thank you," Logan repeated. "Can I see her now?"

"Yes," the doctor answered. "She's been expecting you."

The waiting room held their breath as they watched Logan contemplate. He hadn't been in a place like this in years, and wasn't sure how to respond to his surroundings.

When he turned his head back down the corridor, he saw his younger parents, pacing frantically as he'd been. The same doctor emerged, though younger and with more hair. "Mr. Ramsay, Mrs. Ramsay?" he inquired, tapping his clipboard.

"That's us," Coach Ramsay replied.

"Is our son okay?" Mrs. Ramsay asked.

"Yes and no," the doctor explained. "Physically, it's just some cuts and bruises. They should heal up without any scars in no time."

"And the bad news?" Robert followed up.

"The bad news is," the doctor sighed, "he's manic."

"What do you mean, 'manic'?" Mrs. Ramsay chided. "My son isn't depressed."

"No, not depressed," the doctor clarified, "but he is prone to anxiety attacks, bouts of paranoia, and at times, even vivid hallucinations. His mood can escalate or de-escalate without cause or provocation, but he's especially susceptible to these attacks at moments of great stress."

"So what do we do?" Robert asked. "Make sure

nothing hurts him? He's a kid."

"You'll have to talk him down when an episode occurs."

Mrs. Ramsay shook her head. "How will we know?"

"You'll know."

"Oh thanks," she snapped. "That helps."

"I'm sorry, but you'll likely have to take him to see a psychiatrist. I can give you some referrals if you like."

"We don't need your damn referrals," Mrs. Ramsay hissed. "There's nothing wrong with my son."

"I'll give you two some time," the doctor replied, stepping back and avoiding any more emotional outbursts.

"What are you doing?" Robert asked as she walked toward the exit down the hallway.

"I can't do this," she cried.

"Can't do what?" Robert yelled through his own tears.

"I can't watch my son go through this. I can't see him freak out every time something bad happens, knowing we could be here again."

"We don't have a choice," Robert insisted. "He's our son, and that's our job."

"We *do* have a choice!"

Robert clenched his jaw. "No. We will not do that."

"Then I can't stay," Mrs. Ramsay whispered.

"What do you mean, you can't stay?! That's your son in there!"

"I know I'll never be able to be what he needs," she sniffled. "And you won't, either. You'll see."

"Get the hell out of here," Robert demanded. "Now."

"Robert…"

"You're willing to give up on your four-year-old son because it's inconvenient for you?"

"No," Mrs. Ramsay sobbed. "It's because I know I can't do it, and I know you can't, either."

"Well, even if I can't," Robert gritted, "I'm going to do my damndest to make sure I try."

"And do what, Robert?" Mrs. Ramsay said. "What about when you get called in, or activated, or have drill? What then? You gonna leave him at home by yourself?"

"I'll ask the new neighbors," Robert countered. "The Crows. They seem like nice people, and they have a kid his age. Maybe they'll become friends and watch out for each other."

"And maybe the Browns will win the Super Bowl," muttered Mrs. Ramsay.

"It's not that bad," Robert insisted again.

"It is," Mrs. Ramsay replied, "and you know it as well as I do."

"If you walk out that door," Robert called to her as she again headed for the exit, "don't you dare come back."

Mrs. Ramsay stopped, turning back toward him. "When this inevitably fails, you'll know where to find me."

"Get out!" Robert bellowed before turning around to the door where his son lay. He disappeared inside.

Logan now stood in front of that very door, wishing with all he had that his father would come in there with him once more. He didn't know if he could face this alone, but knew he had to anyway. His mother had doubted him, and he couldn't let her be right, not about this.

He turned the door handle, and it clasped shut behind him, leaving the waiting room in an uncomfortable, tense silence.

Chapter 21

Overcome

"Christ, you look like you just saw a ghost."

Logan resisted the urge to say that technically, he had. It wasn't the time or place to even begin explaining that. His heart was so torn seeing Ellie there, lying in bed. The bruises on her face made him clench his fists in fury, but her eyes still filled with hope kept it at bay.

She laughed at his expression. "What, you've never seen a girl in a hospital before?"

"This isn't funny," he muttered.

"You're telling me. The food is shit, I haven't had a cup of coffee, and everyone keeps looking at I died or something."

"You could've," Logan admitted. "I don't know what they were going to do to you."

"No worse than what they did before you got there,"

she quietly responded. "But no use crying over spilled coffee."

"What is it with you and coffee?"

"I haven't had any fucking coffee, and the headache is killing me!"

"You sure it's not from those bruises?" Logan inquired, then immediately regretted it.

"Shit," she scoffed. "Hope they don't send you to the hospice center next."

"I'm sorry," Logan said, "but it's really hard to see you like this, here."

"Why here?"

"This…" Logan began, then turned away. The combination was way too real.

"Hey!" called Ellie. At attention, he spun back around and looked her in the eye. "Come here."

"I'm right here," he replied.

"Get down here, dammit!"

Logan knelt, doing his best not to stare at her wounds. Several bandages soaked with blood lay at the side of the bed, and it took everything he had not to freak out. Ellie reached out for his hand and grasped it, stronger than what he expected.

"For god's sake, Logan, do I have to walk you through every single step of this?"

"This is the last place I saw my mother," he said at last. The look on Ellie's face indicated her fear that she may have crossed a line this time.

"I'm sorry," she said. "I didn't know it was here. You never talk about it."

"I was four," Logan explained. "What kind of mother leaves her child at four years old?"

"I can't speak to that," Ellie admitted, "but I know that right now, there's nothing in this room for you but love."

"Love, pain, and rage," Logan corrected her. "The cops aren't going to do anything. I doubt they'll even kick those two off the team."

"Of course they won't," snarked Ellie.

"Wait," Logan responded, "what?"

"You think I'm not aware of where I am, where we live, and who we're talking about? Boys can't get raped, right? You can't rape the willing, ha-ha, isn't it hilarious?"

"You're not a boy," Logan insisted.

"To them I am," she muttered. "To them, I always will be."

"You aren't to me," he reiterated. "You're my girlfriend, you're Ellie Crow, and I love you."

Ellie blushed a bit despite herself. "Of course, and I love you too, but don't be naïve, Logan."

"Naïve about what?"

"About the fact that this isn't an isolated incident. About the treatment we're going to get pretty much anywhere we go, even at a place of higher learning like Ohio State. Look at how they're freaking out about gay marriage right now. You really think this country has progressed enough to deal with the trannies and drag queens?"

"I hate that word," Logan mused.

"Either I own it, or it can be used to hurt me," Ellie claimed. "Fuck 'em, they don't deserve it. None of them do."

"You don't, either," he countered.

"Deserve what?"

"This." Logan gestured at the hospital room. "None of this. I'm not going to stop fighting for you."

"For *us*," Ellie corrected.

Logan reached to the hand she was holding and wrapped his other around them both, tears beginning to form in his eyes. "My whole life, people have treated me as Coach Ramsay's son, as a star, a celebrity, someone with a voice…" Logan trailed off, before shaking his head out of a memory and returning. "I'll be damned if I won't use every ounce of that to fight for you, Ellie."

She blushed. "I appreciate that. Don't risk yourself or your life over me, though."

"The hell I won't. I don't care if I have to deal with a Jimmy and Bernie every day—I'm never letting this happen to you again."

"Don't fuck up your scholarship, Ramsay," Ellie snorted, somewhere between an exasperated cry and a laugh. "Last thing we need is to move back home to Orrville and deal with this episode for the rest of our lives."

"I don't care about the scholarship," Logan huffed.

"I do," she insisted. "It's your ticket out of here, away from this shit. I love this little town, but do you really think things are ever going to change here? What, are the Smuckers going to stand up for the trans girls against Pastor Carl?"

"I will," he said.

"I know you will," she laughed.

"I'm serious. Ellie, without you I literally wouldn't be here."

"Logan, don't…"

"No, let me have this one."

Logan released his grip and paced around the room. "I let our differences consume us for years. I made the mistake of worrying about what other people thought, of doing what was the easiest, of not recognizing who had been there for me the whole time and who was just associated with me because I was the coach's son."

He stopped and looked back at Ellie from the end of the bed. "I went with what was comfortable because I wasn't brave enough or educated enough to know what was right, but I do now."

"Logan…"

"Ellie, you're the best thing that's ever happened to me. Not only do I love you with everything I have, but I want to be for you everything you've been to me, and whatever else I can do to assure you of that, I will. You saved my life!"

"And you saved mine," she whispered.

"Wait," Logan stopped, confused. "What?"

"You don't think they were going to do worse once they got the chance?" she asked him. "You think I don't know what a couple of bigots with a vendetta are capable of? You don't think they believe they could get away with murder if they had the balls to do it… excuse the pejorative."

"What?"

"Never mind," she said. "Point is, I might not have made it through if you and Erin hadn't shown up." She stared out the window in the direction of a train whistle far in the distance. "And if they had done what I know they planned, I probably wouldn't have wanted to survive it."

"Don't talk like that."

"It's true!" she said. "This is something that's always

going to be hanging over our heads, Logan. Well, at least mine, if you're not smart enough to get out of this while you can. This is what transgender people always have to deal with in this sick fucking world. We're always looking over our shoulders, we're always ready for the next attack, remark, harassment, judgment, slur, and dirty look."

She broke down in tears, despite herself. "Logan, I'll drag you down. You know it, and I know it. You're going to go off to college, be a star, get drafted, and get out of this. You don't need me distracting you because of the sick fucking douchebags in this world."

"Enough!" Logan said. He leaned down, resting his arms on the railing. "Eleanor, listen to me very carefully."

"My name's Elizabeth."

"Never…" Logan stopped, turning his head. "Wait, really?"

"Yes, Logan. I know my own name."

"Point being," Logan continued after a few seconds, "nothing that I have in this world is worth it if I run away from the person I love more than any of it isn't there with me. The one who loves me despite all my fuck-ups, idiotic decisions, and flaws. Ellie, you're everything to me, and I'm not about to let you suffer because close-minded people don't understand what love can be. You being different has no effect on me, our plans, or anything else."

"You sure?"

"Never been more sure of anything in my life," Logan confirmed.

Ellie wiped her eyes with her sleeve, then summoned him over close. She kissed him on the lips. Logan's cheeks, wet with tears, were beet red.

"Always?" she asked him.

"Always," he reassured her.

Logan finally walked out from the hospital room where everyone stood immediately in anticipation of news.

"How is she?" Josh asked.

"She's okay," Logan answered.

"I hope they lock those two up," muttered Kathy.

Sullenly, he replied, "They're not going to do anything."

"What?" An exasperated cry went up from the room. "They could've killed you!"

"I know," Logan confirmed, looking off into the distance. "But I guess if you're different, you're not a person to some people. How can you assault someone you don't even see as human?"

"We're fighting this," Josh insisted.

"Don't," Logan said.

"Nah, fuck that." Josh further summoned his newfound confidence. "I'm not gonna let this stand."

"What are you gonna do?" Logan asked, rolling his eyes. "Nobody is going to advocate for the removal of our two best defensive players during Wooster week."

"Fuck Wooster!" Josh yelled. "I won't play on a team that embraces people like that and rejects those like you and Ellie."

"None of us will," another teammate echoed.

"I'm not going to let this stand," Josh continued. "Come on, boys. I have an idea."

The rest of the team, ignoring Logan's denial of its necessity, streamed out of the room like the championship trophy awaited on the other side of the door. Logan was left sharing a glance with Erin.

"These boys, when they make up their minds about something," she half-heartedly joked.

"It's a fool's errand," muttered Logan.

"Maybe," she conceded. "But their hearts are in the right place."

"Yeah," he agreed. He started toward the door, a new look of intent gracing his face.

"Where are you going?" called Kathy.

"Let him go," instructed Erin. "He's gonna be fine."

"But..."

Erin smiled. "He's got this."

Chapter 22

Arrival

Logan's cleats clicked against the concrete floor. He paced back and forth outside the locker room, alone, with his jersey in hand. He knew the consequences if this went wrong. He knew what he had to lose, but at that moment, it didn't seem to matter a whole lot. If standing up for what was right meant that the Bucks didn't want him, he didn't want to go there, anyway. If standing up for what was right meant he'd be ostracized from Orrville, then he didn't want to live there.

If the world wasn't ready to accept his love for Ellie, not to mention what should be right and just in this world, then he would fight with all he had until it was.

The band had already started. The stretches were complete, and the fans were in the stands. The jeers from the Wooster side were almost as deafening. Logan expected it to be a microcosm of what the atmosphere might be the first time he went to Ann Arbor.

It was nothing compared to what awaited him in the locker room, and he was aware of that too.

Finally, he turned the steel handle, and with a deep sigh, stepped forth, ready to embrace his destiny. Whatever that might be, it was now or never.

Clack. Clack. Clack. Every step he took echoed against the concrete blocks that lined his path. Shadows started to block out the light of his steps, and his head arose to see his Red Rider teammates standing on each side, creating a tunnel within a tunnel that led to the center of the locker room. Each one of them nodded and smacked his shoulders as he passed, and they started clapping slowly as he reached the center of the main dressing area.

There, in the center, was his father's old stool. The one that sat near his desk, the one that hadn't been used since he left, the one on which his father stood before the last time Orrville won a state championship. The body language from the players surrounding him indicated that it was his turn to be the Ramsay on the Rise.

"Father, I hope you'll hear me one day," he whispered. He took one moment of hesitation to acknowledge the heaviness of the event, and then stood atop his team.

As he peered down at the sea of red that gathered around him, his head became more clear than it had ever before. His own mental Red Sea parted, allowing thoughts and clarity to penetrate through the protective filters than he realized was possible. It was an epiphany. It was his moment. It was time to make the final stand.

"Red Riders," he began, barely a tremble in his voice despite the butterflies in his stomach, "out there, we face our storybook rival. Out there, Wooster is ready to avenge their loss to us. Out there, half the people who have gathered are clamoring for their Cinderella story to be completed. Out there..." He trailed off, his eyes connecting with each player his eyes caught.

"Out there, we will conduct ourselves as a team the way Orrville High Red Riders are expected to. When we face Wooster, we will conduct ourselves with sportsmanship, respect, intensity, dedication, and valor..." Several of the Red Riders cheered in agreement. "And we will conduct ourselves with class."

His eyes turned to the corner where he knew they were standing. He knew they were gazing upon him. He knew inside their brains, and whatever conscience they may have left, they acknowledged what they had gotten away with.

There they were, faces smug and arms crossed. Bernie, Jimmy—those faces he'd known so long, had grown up with, and once considered friends. Those faces that now bore only the memory of pain, strife, violence, and outright despicable acts. No matter how tough he was, it was impossible to not be adversely affected by the knowing stares of two giants capable of such dastardly deeds.

"There are two of you, two of our teammates," he stated calmly but intentionally in their direction, "who have not lived up to these virtues." He stepped down off the stool, and a path parted directly toward that corner. He took a deep breath, prepared for anything, and stepped forward. One at a time, one pace, one stride, one anything could lead to his entire life changing in an instant, but he did it anyway. He stopped right before the corner, where

Bernie and Jimmy weren't fazed whatsoever.

"These two teammates have disgraced my Father's name. These two teammates have soured the reputation of Red Rider football. These two teammates…" He stopped and then grabbed both of them by the collar of their jerseys and pulled them forward. "These two teammates violated someone's consent, and resorted to violence in the face of disagreement."

"Get the fuck off me, Ramsay," Bernie demanded while shoving him.

"We got off," Jimmy added. "The cops won't arrest us, and there's nothing you can do about it."

"Oh?" Logan's face lit up. "There isn't? There isn't *anything* I can do?"

"No, Ramsay," Jimmy affirmed. "Now quit wasting our time. Go play with your boyfriend or something."

"Yeah, queer-loving faggot," Bernie agreed. "Why don't you get off this team? Nobody wants to be in this locker room with your eyes scanning the other guys while they're undressing, right, boys?"

Nobody made a sound. Logan turned to the side, contemplative and confident, then returned to the spot on his stool. "That's what you're going with?"

"Yeah," Bernie shouted.

"Now are you gonna shut up already so we can go play football?" Jimmy inquired.

"That's a very good question," Logan confirmed. "Are we going to go play football right now? I mean, we should, right? The fans are here, the bands are here, and we're scheduled to run out of that tunnel in about three minutes. What ever should we do, Riders?"

The team remained silent. Jimmy and Bernie grew

frustrated and started toward the stool. Like a machine, the Red Riders closed the path.

"What the fuck?" Jimmy squealed.

"Get out of the way!" screamed Bernie. "Don't tell me you're on board with this faggot too!"

"Bernie, Jimmy," Logan sternly responded, "get the fuck out of this locker room, and never come back."

Bernie and Jimmy looked at each other, and then burst out laughing. "Yeah right!" Bernie guffawed.

"Like you have the power to kick us off this team!" Jimmy added.

"I don't have the power to kick you off, no," Logan conceded. "But I will say this: If you don't take off those jerseys and immediately leave this locker room, never to return, I'm not going out there."

"Good!" Bernie chided. "We don't need you, anyway!"

"Right!" Jimmy started to chime in, but then whispered to Bernie, "Actually we would. He's pretty good."

"Shut up," Bernie stage-whispered back.

"No, seriously," Jimmy insisted. "He scored all the points last time. I don't think we'd win without him."

"Jimmy!" Bernie shouted, elbowing him in the stomach. Bernie then turned toward the team.

"Well, let's go, then. Which of you are gonna take this traitor's side, and which of you are going to take the field with the real men in the room? Men who do what they want, take what they want, and kick some ass. Who's with me?"

"We don't side with rapists," a new voice said.

"Who said that?" Bernie called back.

Josh stepped from behind the lockers and in front of Logan. When he crossed his arms, the rest of the team did the same in full cohesion, each one of them staring down Jimmy and Bernie with utter disdain.

"Are you serious right now?" Jimmy gasped.

"Dead serious," Josh confirmed. "Either we run out of that tunnel, or you two do, and you can go forfeit the game. Your call."

"We don't forfeit!" Bernie exclaimed. "And we're not rapists!"

"You're not?" Josh snickered. "Why not?"

"You can't rape a dude," Jimmy explained.

"So you're saying you did violate Ellie?" Josh pressed.

"Of course we did," Jimmy replied. Bernie tried elbowing him again, but to no avail. "Why wouldn't we? If he wants to be a she so badly, we'll treat her like it."

Bernie tried covering Jimmy's mouth with a glove. "Shut up, dammit!"

"Why?" Jimmy asked, feigning cluelessness. "We do it all the time!"

"Goddammit, Jimmy," Bernie muttered, walking away from his lifelong friend and only ally in this fight.

"What?" Jimmy challenged the rest of them. "Like you guys never have."

Logan again jumped off the chair, and stomped up to Jimmy, looking him dead in the face. "None of us are the sick fucking bastards you two are. You're never going to touch my girlfriend again."

"Oh?" Jimmy shoved him confidently. "And how are you going to do that?"

Logan's head turned toward the door at the end of the locker room that he'd come in. At that moment, the door opened, and the two Orrville police officers walked in.

"Aw, what?" Jimmy protested.

"They set us up, you fucking idiot," snarled Bernie.

"Why don't you come on down to the station with us," the tall officer suggested. "I'd like to hear very much about these supposed acts you do all the time."

"I'd like to hear that too," confirmed the shorter officer. "Now, you boys," he added, turning to the team, "you go get us into States. We'll take care of these two."

"Go, Red Riders?" Logan suggested.

"Go, Red Riders!" the rest of the team shouted in unison.

They burst forth from the locker room, screaming at the top of their lungs as the field awaited their presence. Each of them started smacking their helmets together and firing each other up. Logan stood by with Josh until Coach Stewert appeared in front of them.

"Logan?" he called out.

"Yes, Coach Stewert?"

"Why don't you lead us out?" he asked.

Logan shook his head.

"What do you mean, no?" Coach exasperatedly responded. "You got what you wanted, didn't you?"

Logan turned to Josh and grabbed him by the helmet. "You lead us out, Josh."

"What?" Josh, completely caught off guard, shook his head. "No! I can't do that!"

"We might be dead if it weren't for you," Logan reminded him. "Take us out, Josh. Boys?"

The entire team cheered again in support as Josh jumped to the front of the team. Like a kid on Christmas morning, he beamed at the rest of his teammates. "Are we ready?"

"Yeah!"

"Let's go!" he yelled, turning toward the field at a full sprint.

They broke through the Orrville banner the cheerleaders held up, and an extremely loud cheer arose from the Orrville side of the stadium. The fight song echoing in his ears as they ran toward the sideline, Logan finally felt lighter than he had in years. The only thing missing was…

"Here to announce our ceremonial coin toss, school paper editor, Ellie Crow!"

"What?" Logan stammered in surprise.

"Dude, go," Josh urged. "Trust me!"

Ellie stood in front of the color guard, each of them firmly carrying an American flag. Logan jogged out to Ellie, hugging her tenderly so as not to hurt her further.

"What are you doing here?" he inquired after releasing.

"I wouldn't miss it for the world!"

"You're going to flip the coin?"

"No, I'm here to announce it," Ellie explained. "But I think…" She motioned behind him. "…you should see for yourself."

From the Orrville tunnel, the military standard appeared in full step. The drums accompanied their precise movement, their flags flapping in the wind. They marched toward the center of the field, not breaking formation for a second, until they came to attention on the forty-yard line. Then, they parted, and one of them removed their cap.

"Father?" Logan cried out in jubilation.

The old soldier stepped out from the shadows and confirmed it. Logan would recognize that smile anywhere.

He ran the distance and nearly toppled his father completely. The soldiers of the standard saluted in respect, and the crowd went insane.

"Ladies and gentlemen," Ellie's said over the PA, "please welcome back Coach Robert Ramsay!"

"U-S-A! U-S-A!" the crowd unanimously chanted.

"Son," Robert laughed as he pried Logan's hands away. "You've got a game to go win!"

"We thought you were…"

"Nah," Robert playfully responded, "nobody would ever make me break my promise."

"Which promise?"

"That I'd always come home to you, son," Robert explained with a smile.

Logan hugged his father in pure elation one more time, and then Robert directed him back toward the fifty-yard line for the toss.

Ellie's face lit up the night. "Go on," Robert encouraged Logan. "This should've happened years ago."

He looked to his father for confirmation. "Go!" Robert repeated, shoving him toward her.

Logan stumbled toward Ellie, tears of happiness streaming down his face. "You knew about this?"

"I told you, I'd do anything to make you happy, Logan," she confirmed. "I love you."

"I love you!" he proclaimed, then kissed her passionately while everyone clapped. They might've stood surrounded by thousands of football fans, his father, his team, and the entire world for that matter, but in that small moment of ecstasy, love, and pure affection, Logan and

Ellie may as well have been alone anywhere in the galaxy—
for their love transcended football, fear, gender, and life
itself. It was always meant to be that way, after all. It just
got off to a—

A false start.

Post-Script Essays

Stay

Lucinda Lugeons

I met Marissa after her appearance on the *God Awful
Movies* podcast, and she quickly turned into one of my go-
to friends over Messenger. I had the pleasure of meeting
her in person in Chicago at a live show, and immediately
found in her both a kindred spirit and a new friend.

When she first asked me to write an essay for her
new book, I agreed almost instinctively, although I wasn't
sure I would have anything of substance to include. But
she was kind enough to share *False Start* with me as she
was writing it; and as I read the story of Logan and Ellie, I
found myself in deep sympathy with Logan and those
around him who didn't understand the struggles he
experienced on a daily basis. I sympathized because I have
lived it, though to a smaller degree to be sure.

You see, I grew up with a mentally ill mother. And
for me, that meant growing up with a mother who often
left when things got hard. Of course, when I was a kid, I
didn't get it. She must not love me enough to stay, right? I
must have done something to push her away, right? It
must be me, because she *looks* fine. She doesn't look any

different than anybody else's mom. I didn't get it.

As I grew older and started to understand the world more (and, more relevantly, started to understand *myself* more), I found that I also understood her more. I struggled with my own brand of anxiety and depression, and along the way it helped me to comprehend her struggles. But I also learned more about her absences. And sure, sometimes when she went away, she went and lived life alone, in another city for a fresh start, to regroup. But, as I found out later, other times she went to live in a mental hospital until she felt safe enough to return to us.

And she deserves my gratitude for that. And for the fact that despite a lifetime of struggling with her illness, she always came back to try again. She was strong, and I know now that she fought hard every day to stay.

I was only nineteen years old when we lost her. A lifetime of self-destructive behavior, and a tendency to take much better care of others than she did herself finally caught up with her. And I miss her every day.

Mental illness can't be seen at a glance, it can't be sniffed out. It can, however, be understood if we just take the time to do so. On the surface, you can't see the turmoil within but one thing my mom taught me is this: Never stop trying to understand. Never give up on yourself or those you love. Always come back.

I remind myself of this like a mantra when I feel myself slipping. When my palms get sweaty and my heart races and I feel like my skin is crawling off for no apparent reason, I tell myself over and over to come back; to stay. I tell myself to be strong and to face this head on. I recognize how lucky I am to have a husband whose rationality and understanding help to keep me grounded, and I know that not everyone has somebody like that. But everyone *can* be someone like that.

The point of this rambling bit of autobiography is really simple: Whether you're dealing with your own mental illness, or the illness of someone you love, stay strong. Stay hopeful. Stay empathetic. Stay grounded. Stay you.

Above all, stay. And if you can't do that, never give up, never stop fighting, and always, *always* come back.

Medical Records and Memories as a Winter Landscape

Tanya Simpson

Seeing your own medical records feels surprisingly impersonal.

Maybe it's because some details fell off the edge when you moved from one part of town to another and had to register with a different doctor because you were no longer in the right catchment area for your previous one.

Maybe it's because there was a clear severing of your past from your current life when you moved from one country to another and notes from doctors and hospitals didn't travel with you.

Maybe it's the small inaccuracies, the moment when one eating disorder became labelled as another because of a typing error or a missed word somewhere along the way, and ED-NOS with features of both bulimia and anorexia became bulimia-on-its-own, which you never actually had. Even now the concept of binging makes your heart thud against your ribs, because your purging in a past life took the form of an attempt to rid yourself of what you actually were, not what you had consumed.

Or maybe it's the sensation of seeing, in black and white, the progression from an observation of symptoms to a diagnosis to a chronic primary something-or-other, as the confusion of your body overtook the confusion of your mind before your mind eventually followed suit, and you were given an opportunity to learn new acronyms for your self-destructive coping mechanisms.

Maybe it's because when you were handed sheets of paper that contained this information, it was easier to believe that you were reading about someone else instead of feeling guilty for the body that survived everything you put it through.

But when you finally decided to give it freedom, it chose instead to exist in a perpetual state of dysfunction.

It's so easy to give in to the misconception that your body did this as an act of revenge, to spite you, rather than to accept the mundane truth—that there is only so much damage that can be caused by injuries and viruses before the situation goes from "when you get better" to *"if* you get better," to the alternative that doesn't bear thinking about.

You remember your last session with the one, good therapist when you were twenty or twenty-one, and he read out loud his notes from your first session and asked how you felt about that person. You said, "That's not me. That's someone else," and he thought you meant it because you had become so much stronger, but you actually meant it because you had never been able to relate other people's explanations of what you were and how you might have become those things.

You meant it because for all your self-awareness, you had never wanted to believe how far you had fallen. You still don't.

Now the fractures and blunt force traumas of your past life and the details of the times you lost yourself have been erased, and you are left with only a few short years of history to comprehend.

It still shakes you to your core, a place you once believed was populated with strength above all else. You tell yourself stories of things that are more beautiful for having been broken, but you don't believe a word you say. You have learned to accept the scars on the outside, even as new ones have appeared, even as you have put them there yourself, but you cannot forgive the scars on the inside and what they have turned you into.

You do not hate yourself. Instead, you are disgusted. You start to list the ways in which you are still strong, still determined, but it turns into a list of ways that this is somehow all your fault and you can never build high enough walls to contain yourself.

You remember the physiotherapist who told you that you had to learn to stop because your body couldn't handle what you were doing to it in the name of making miracles happen, and you remember being so scared of stopping in case you were never able to start again.

You also remember the ex-professional boxer you met at the physio centre who strapped your hands into gloves then put on boxing pads and told you to hit him until you felt better. Even though you could hardly stand up, you punched and punched until he was taking steps backwards to lessen the force of your rage.

When you were doubled over, gasping for breath and the world became dark around the edges, you finally felt better.

He said, "You're very angry."

You said, "I know."

It didn't cross your mind that this wasn't a positive thing, but it surprised you that, for once, someone else noticed. It also didn't cross your mind that angry was something you had every reason to be, because anger is hot and loud and you are ice and silence.

You slide another copy of your medical records into another envelope to send to another government office and welcome the familiar freeze that creeps in around your edges, the brittle frost that allows you not to feel. Now the memories of how your body and mind were twisted and warped have become a cold garden of bare trees that you stumble through, arms wrapped around yourself in apology as you try not to take up space.

You stare at the ground and still your breath as a dead branch cracks underfoot and the sound splits the air like a gunshot.

Tanya Simpson is a writer, photographer, and coffee drinker living in Edinburgh, Scotland, and can be found online at tanyasimonesimpson.com.

I Was That Guy

Matt Briner

I was that guy.

Y'know, *that guy.*

When Ris started coming out a few years ago, I was at her place. There were a few of us, and she and another friend were talking about her feelings and the whole process of coming out and transition and the opposition she was facing, and I was the dumbass who said, "Can't you just be [you]?"

Except I didn't say "[you]." I said her birth name, now called her "deadname."

The reason I used her birth name is because, honestly, she hadn't told me her real name yet; I had known her by this name for a year and a half at that point, and I thought she'd just keep going by that.

But Ris hates her deadname with a fire to match a million suns. In a small way, it's a shame because it was an awesome name, but since it's associated with such brutal memories, it's become completely tainted and should never be used again. The exact same thing happened to the word "twilight."

Her response was blunt, more so than I was used to from her by that point: "No. I'm not him. I'm Marissa."

And so, I met my friend for the second time.

It took her a while to discover that, emotionally, she was in no way male. For a while, she was "bigender," then "gender fluid," then maybe a few other things. I think she was doing this to hold on to the last vestiges of hope that she could please everybody in some way.

Then she met Pastor Carl (yeah, the character in the book is based on a real guy, and the interaction is on YouTube, in case you haven't seen it) and whatever grip she had on that feeling of "I want to please everyone" was released.

I don't think of that as Marissa's birth, because she's always been a girl; I think of it as her male persona's death. The prison that she felt trapped in her entire life, the feeling of dependence on the approval of others and the desire for acceptance, crumbled like wet cardboard when "I'm transgender; *fuck you!*" left her lips that day in Philadelphia.

Since I met her the first time in January of 2013, I haven't seen anyone as busy, vocal, or determined as Marissa McCool. In that time, she's held several jobs, each with its own personal level of soul-crushing Hell. She worked at Joseph A Bank, which provided her with retail stress, customer frustration, and so goddamned much Christmas music that she despises it to this day despite having not worked there for over two years now.

She worked for a local bakery as a deliverer, a job she absolutely loved because she absolutely loves driving, and it helped that the bakery was owned by a very close friend. You can imagine then the surprise when she came home from a ten-day vacation in Minnesota to discover that the bakery had closed down without notice, and you can imagine the blood-boiling rage and sadness in her heart when her boss refused to hand over her last paycheck, something that, to my knowledge, is still in litigious limbo.

(As an aside, Ris was kind enough to get me an interview at that bakery after I had graduated from university. It was for an accounting position there, and the owner balked at my salary recommendation even though it was standard for a newly-graduated accountant, not to mention fully negotiable. A few days later, Ris told me that he had chewed her out for bringing me in. Maybe if he had used the $35,000 he'd spent on a shiny new website to pay me to work for him, he'd have discovered that $25,000 is too fucking much to pay on one-time website design.)

She's worked as an Uber driver, which again, she introduced me to, and I've been a driver ever since. Ris, however, didn't hold onto it because she found it to be dangerous, draining work, and she had enough on her plate. I don't blame her for leaving considering how badly under fire Uber has become in recent months. Me, I'm a masochist, so I'm still hanging around.

Through all this, since I've known her, she's also had a YouTube show, she's hosted three different podcasts (two of which are still on the air), she's written multiple short films with a few more that were left incomplete for one reason for another, she's written two books on top of the six or seven that she had already written under her deadname, she has two children of whom she has since taken custody and given a better home, and she's spent four years getting three degrees from the University of Pennsylvania, an Ivy League school with a 9.4% acceptance rate who thought Ris was so remarkable that they let her in despite the fact that she didn't finish high school.

Meanwhile, I get winded just tying my shoes and have never held a job longer than twenty-three months.

Despite all this, Ris still has to prove herself to our society, whereas I don't. As a perfect example, the other day, I was driving two Uber customers back to their dorm when I was pulled over on account of a busted brake light. This was at Penn State University in State College, Pennsylvania. More than that, it was an unofficial holiday called "State Patty's Day," a day that students use to get as plastered as possible the weekend before Spring Break begins because Penn State pays off all the local bars to close down on St. Patrick's Day every year (but some intrepid students did the math and realized that Penn State couldn't do this every weekend, so the tradition began; besides, St. Patrick's Day still gets pretty good business).

Anyway, my point is that, despite it being a hellacious night for Uber drivers and policemen alike, this cop let me off with a friendly verbal warning. Didn't even give me a ticket. Now, maybe it's just because it was for a brake light and none of us were drunk or causing any real trouble— after all, it was a white male cop, I'm a white male driver, and it was a college town.

The issue is that I honestly don't know how differently it would have gone if any of those factors were different. If Ris were driving instead of me, who knows how differently that would have gone? Would she have gotten a ticket? Would she have been asked to step out of the car? Would she have been harassed?

That lack of assurance bothers me, as it should bother literally everybody. The stink of inequality permeates our country and our world, and every time you turn around, you see people getting treated differently based on mood. In the example I just provided (the first time getting pulled over for a blown-out brake light), everybody should be given one free pass, but we all know that's not true.

We all know that blacks are pulled over more often than whites (13% in 2011 as opposed to 10% according to the Bureau of Justice Statistics; that data was recording "being stopped at least once"), that they're incarcerated more for lesser charges (their sentences are, on average, 20% longer, according to the American Civil Liberties Union), and that the prison population is disproportionate as it relates to race (according to the Bureau of Prisons, 37.9% of federal inmates as of December 2016 are black despite black people making up only 13% of the population).

For trans people? According to the Office for Victims of Crime within the U.S. Department of Justice, 50% of all trans people are sexually assaulted at some point in their lifetime. (Even one person is shameful enough, but there are an estimated 1.4 million transgender adults in the United States, making up 0.6% of the population, and half of them have been sexually assaulted.) Of those 700,000 people, 15% report it happening in police custody, and 32% of those people are reportedly black. What's worse, anywhere from 5% to 9% of those 700,000 were assaulted sexually by a police officer.

What all this means is that, what was a routine, friendly traffic stop for me (a white male) could end up becoming an unnecessary inconvenience (or much, much worse) to another person just because they're not white, or fully male. What is a trip to the men's gas station bathroom for me could end up becoming the most traumatic experience of another person's life just because they don't have a penis, and I didn't even get into the bathroom statistics because there's nothing to talk about and trans people don't want to hurt you so let shitters shit, okay?!

I've been in a public bathroom with Ris and the worst thing she did was take a piss. What do you think she's gonna do when she's in there, eat cake at you?! You think her husband, Aiden, is going to accost anyone in the men's bathroom at Sheetz? I have news for you—anyone who's seen what Ris looks like knows that any of the guys in that bathroom are a *massive* downgrade.

The point that I'm taking *far* too long to make is that I don't have to worry nearly as much as Ris, or any trans person, does. I'm concerned on a daily basis that her daily commute to the University of Pennsylvania will end badly in one way or another simply because she's trans and out. Nobody should have to go through what she does, getting yelled at by radical pastors simply because she's different, or having ignorant assholes insist on referring to her with male pronouns because she has a dick (like they'd know or it's their business), much less worry about not getting home that night.

There's no excuse for the way trans people are treated by the bigoted jackasses of the world: upbringing is no excuse because even the most uneducated guy in the grungiest, poorest town in America can understand what the word "different" means and accept it; ignorance is no excuse because anyone who's ever said "What should I tell my kids?" has no defense anymore because you can just Google "What should I tell my kids?", and religious belief is no excuse because any god that demands hatred toward and exclusion of anybody simply because they're different is a god that doesn't deserve worship, and I personally would rather go to Hell than spend an eternity in that god's presence.

Anyone who speaks to Ris for five minutes loves her to death (believe me, I speak from experience). They know her as an intelligent, sweet, beautiful, creative person, a devoted wife and mother, and an obnoxiously hard worker. She loves her husband, her children, trains, and cake. She tolerates professional wrestling and reads books like she'll die if she stops. She knows more about the American Civil War than I know about myself, and she's been known to walk miles a day just to take pictures of abandoned train rails. She talks about trains all day, she giggles when she sees a train, she dreams about trains…

This. Girl. Fucking. Loves. Trains.

Except Amtrak.

Fuck Amtrak.

The bottom line, assuming you've read this far along, is that I am insanely jealous of Marissa McCool, and that jealousy would burn me to the soul if I didn't love her deeply for who she is.

Regardless of what's in her pants.

Regardless of whether or not she's wearing makeup.

Regardless of whether or not she's wearing her cosmic design leggings today.

Regardless of whichever of the eleventy bajillion podcasts she's listening to today.

Regardless of whichever of the forteenthy galillion

books she's got her nose buried in today.
    Regardless of what her name is.
    I'm jealous of Ris because she's Ris.
    I love Ris because she's Ris.
    And if you don't, you're wrong.

When Everyone Means Everyone

Christin Kapp

I cried through church today.

This is not all that an uncommon occurrence, though it hasn't happened in a good long while...which was nice.

My dry eye streak ended this morning.

And I wasn't even wearing waterproof mascara.

Shit.

I have a lot on my mind lately, with the election looming, and fighting for the passage of Carlisle's non-discrimination ordinance, and gearing up for the holidays... and that doesn't even scratch the personal crap going through my busy little brain on a daily basis.

Sometimes, a good cry is cathartic.

Sometimes, it's necessary.

And sometimes, you cry because you realize that you missed an opportunity to live out your worldview/faith/beliefs, and you're kicking yourself in the ass for fucking up and not living up to your own theology.

And *that* was what sent me over the edge into a

puddle of pew-tears this morning.

I fucked up.

Last night, I had an opportunity to live out the core of my belief system—that every person on this planet has inherent dignity and worth, and should be treated accordingly, even if you disagree or don't see eye to eye—and I didn't act that way.

Believing it is easy. Living it is harder.

If you follow me at all on social media, you'll know that I've been very vocal at city council meetings in regards to our local anti-discrimination ordinance. It would guarantee the rights of all Carlisle's residents (particularly Carlisle's LGBTQIA residents), and it needs to be passed.

There's a particular member of our city council who has been more than slightly opposed to this piece of legislation, and she's made her disdain for LGB, and especially T, people plain during council meetings, to the point that I called her out by name at the last meeting for her rude behavior while sitting on the council bench, asking her to put her phone away and actually pay attention when we speak.

She boils my blood.

And she showed up at my church's annual charity auction last night.

Yep.

Ms. "I don't think discrimination exists, LGBTQ people don't need equal rights, I'm going to play on my phone while transpeople talk so I don't have to listen to them" showed up to a charity auction at a Unitarian Universalist church.

Oh, the irony.

She was surrounded by the very people she is

refusing to include and protect.

She was invited by a member of the congregation.

And I was *pissed*.

My first thought, upon seeing her, was *What the hell is that woman doing invading the one queer-friendly church in this town?!*

She'd invaded my sacred space. Brought the fight, just with her presence, to the place I consider my sanctuary from all the fighting.

If I hadn't been emceeing the event, I would have bolted. I didn't want to be in the same room with her.

And then, as I sat seething behind the set on the stage, I had a realization that gave me a swift kick right in the conscience.

I heard the words of our first principle in my mind...

"We affirm the dignity and worth of every human being"

And I heard Aija's voice, as she greets us every Sunday—

"You are welcome here. You are needed here. You are wanted here."

And that meant her too.

Even her.

Especially her.

I wish I could say that I came off the stage and greeted her. Welcomed her to the auction. Welcomed her to UUCV. Told her that I hoped she had a good time. Offered her a glass of wine.

But I didn't.

I had an opportunity to live out that central tenant of my faith, and I blew it.

Instead, I sat on the stage, hoping she didn't see me, repeating, "Everyone means everyone. Inherent dignity and worth means everyone," over and over like a mantra.

Near the end of the night, I looked around the room.

She was gone.

And it was then that I felt that kick in the guts feeling.

You know what I succeeded in doing?

I made myself miserable trying to avoid her all night, *and* I didn't do anything to make her feel welcome.

I've been stewing about it ever since.

If *anyone* in the history of ever needed to walk through our doors, it was her.

She needed to see us all there, feel what inclusion, what radical welcome feels like.

Maybe it wouldn't have changed anything.

But maybe it would have.

And I had the opportunity to be part of that change.

And I blew it.

I wish I could say that I got it right. That I live out my faith perfectly every time.

But I don't.

And I royally missed the mark on this one.

And now I have to figure out where to go from here.

Faith can be a messy thing, especially when it's a faith that is an orthopraxy, and is more about how we treat ourselves and others than in belief in a divine being.

I didn't get it right this time. I'm trying not to be too hard on myself for that.

So I had a good cry.

And if I see her in the grocery, I'm going to say hello… and mean it.

An Outside Perspective
Fred Sims

I am an outsider. I have no mental health issues. I am probably one of the least qualified people to offer a selection for this book.

But I also have a wife who suffers from anxiety. "Suffers" probably isn't even the correct nomenclature. I should probably say she *lives* with anxiety. Nomenclature be damned, I see how the anxiety affects my wife every day. I see her battling herself over every decision. Decisions about money, decisions about her health, even decisions about what side to have with dinner. She suffers. Don't get me wrong, she sees her doctor and routinely takes the meds prescribed her. Still, she suffers.

I love my wife dearly. She embodies all the pieces I am missing. Where I lack empathy, she picks up the slack. When I'm goofy, she pats me on the head and says, "I love you." When I rage and rant, she listens. When I am quiet and introspective, she joins me in silent vigil.

I don't want to present my wife as solely just an extension of myself; she isn't *just* the person who completes me. That is an odd sentence for me to type. Not because of the fact that my wife isn't just an extension of me, but the thought of what that means. She is so important to me; such a part of everything I do, say, or think that it is hard to distinguish us from one another at times.

What I do know for certain is that my wife cares about everyone, and I don't mean that in a hyperbolic way either. She cares about everyone. She doesn't need to know you. She doesn't need to like you. She cares anyway. This is a woman who enjoys her independence; reading a good book, or losing herself in a game or twelve of solitaire. She loves to travel and explore especially on lazy Sundays together. Most important is the caring though, it is what sets her apart from anyone I have ever met.

We can discuss anything—we *have* discussed anything. There is nothing I wouldn't do for my wife.

That is why I try to help her, even though I am woefully inexperienced when it comes to the care people with mental health issues require. I'm not talking about from doctors, either—I just mean the care from the people around them; from those who care about them. Because of her anxiety, there is a daily chance my wife will have a panic attack or burst into tears for what I perceive as an undefinable reason. Me not seeing the reason in no way invalidates her feelings, but this is my honest appraisal of how I hope I help and so it feels important to state that I sometimes can't connect with what is driving her anxiety.

It is difficult to put myself in her shoes. I can't know what she is experiencing, or the depth of her pain. I probably do all the wrong things every time, but I combat her anxiety the best way I can think of: head-on. In my mind, there is no other recourse, because the excruciating nature of her illness is more than I can bear. Although I am an integral part of her life, I'm not involved in this battle just because—as someone who loves her and deeply empathizes with her—her struggle impacts me. What's far more important, and what is a far worthier goal, is that she deserves relief, understanding, and someone who puts in the work solely for her benefit, all other reasons and attachments aside.

And so I get to work.

When she seems sad, I work on making her laugh. It's not hard; I'm ridiculous, and all it really takes is for me to say the word "pooper." That is a cheap laugh, though, and she deserves more work from me, so I try and stay on my game at all times.

When her feelings are lying to her and telling her she is the worst person that ever existed, I am stern. I let her know that notion is a lie, that not one person in her life that matters could ever feel that way, and I reiterate exactly how much I love her and what she means to me. There are days I must repeat this multiple times. But because I know it helps, I am content to say these things as many times as they need saying. If she required it, I would be an endless loop of positive words for her.

When she feels buried by work, where the money from her next paycheck is going, or even just by the thought of a totally free Sunday with no pre-made plans, I am the calming voice telling her to take it one breath/step/day at a time.

I do these things not because of obligation but because I want to. I suffer from that age-old, slightly misogynistic delusion that I need to be her knight in shining armor. She deserves someone who will be steadfast through all her ups and downs, a stalwart she can turn to at any time and say, "There you are, you're still here."

One of the most rewarding payoffs of all this is that she trusts me. She doesn't like expressing her feelings, always afraid she doesn't have the words. She lets me drag it out of her, trusts me to help her talk things out/down/in circles. It is the least I can do to try and be the best husband I can.

I am writing this, despite how it may read, for her and not me. I am not looking for adulation or pats on the back. I am attempting to open my brain and really share our interaction so she always has a place to look and see how I feel. Her feelings may lie to her, or her anxiety may get the best of her, but I will never stop being there to fight back with her. I will never stop being there to gently take her hand and hold it through those times when the lack of words frustrates her to tears. I will never stop being there for the best hugs in all the world.

I write this as a surprise, so she can see that no matter what those intrusive thoughts say, she is beautiful, amazing, sweet, funny, worthwhile, wanted, loved, needed, and all the other adjectives that would be in this list if I was smart enough to remember them.

I am an outsider, but every day, I fight for the love of my life so she can see that her anxiety does not define her. It is difficult at times, downright frustrating at others. Despite that, I will never stop.

I love you, Ren. Every bit of you, exactly as you are. Now come give me a hug, because I know what reading this has done, and I'm here...

Post-Script: Becoming Marissa

Marissa Alexa McCool

Introduction

A journey is not always where we go, but how we get there, and the destination is not always something tangible.

This collection of essays travels, written during the semester I came out, along with my wandering mind as much as it does multiple locations. I entered this semester strung out, stressed out, and limping to the finish line, and now will leave it differently than I arrived for a multitude of reasons. The main one was finally being open about myself to others at the university, and these writings were done in a space that was made available to me to articulate this.

I always knew I was different, I just didn't know why. The guidance of this writing class changed me forever, as I got in touch with that girl inside dying to scream out, but the filter wasn't broken in that spot. It was at the Bent Button, as I was kept from class by arguing with a Hate Pastor. The epiphany that washed over me was one that forever changed my journey at the University of Pennsylvania, even as it nears completion.

"I'm transgender, fuck you!" I screamed in his face after pretending to allow him to judge me for five minutes captured on film. It was a release, a cathartic burst of honesty that helped kick-start my public transition. The election results sealed it for good, though. After testing the waters when class was on Halloween, the way I was treated by my classmates made me feel safe, at least there. Six weeks later, my name is changed as far as the University is concerned, and I walk into every class looking how I feel instead of how I used to think I needed to.

I'll never forget what this class has done for me, which is why I dedicated the book to all of them. Oh yeah, I wrote a book in nine days after the election as my coming-out piece. I didn't so much come out of the closet as much as I did kick it down and dare anyone to object. I have never felt stronger, happier, and more content with who I am, and I became a voice for so many who cannot speak up right now. It's been life-changing, but for the better.

Through a series of very simple prompts, my words came from Franklin Field, the Schuylkill Pike, and scenes from a memory. My travels are only beginning, and I look forward to where they take the real me.

Observing Franklin Field

My heavy black boots press in the soft surface where grass once stood strong, living, and growing. Now artificial turf carries the thundering footsteps of cleats. Surrounding it are bricks and aluminum seats, carrying the stories of over one hundred years of hopes, dreams, failures, and prominence. The closed gridiron becomes blue paint beneath my weathered feet, and across my mind wander all the great athletes who scored six points by stepping there. I think of how the empty bleachers were once filled to capacity for the native sons of Philadelphia. The Quakers as a national athletic powerhouse left that potential behind in 1954, and will likely never return to it.

That isn't a sad story, however. Those who seek fame and fortune by playing a game will enroll elsewhere, but soon a few dozen good-hearted kids will charge the field before their friends, family, and few others. They're held to the same standard the rest of the students are, unlike the major Universities where they're basically semi-professional. Five thousand may watch their charge to football glory, but those who work within these walls know them for their quality and not necessarily their future draft number. I can't help but prefer that to the celebrity status athletes are given at other D-1 schools.

I prepare to start the ninety-three-row climb to the top of Franklin Field, where I'll record practice for the coaches. As I glance around at the empty seats, the cheers that once resounded within this building permeate its vacant corridors. These concrete steps increase the stress on my calf muscles a little less than they have every other time for the last year-plus. Not to mention, chasing field goals from the kickers hasn't hurt my endurance either.

At the top of the first section, I turn once more toward the gridiron where pads will soon be crunching and sweat will drip like the dew that moistened its surface hours earlier. I can't help but reflect on how I got here. I was hired for a college football team as a thirty-one-year-old artsy kid, the granddaughter of the great Roger Farr who was enshrined in the local and state hall-of-fame for spending years teaching his own kids athletic and scholarly excellence. As one who never received much sentiment from either branch of their own family tree, I feel a certain kinship with this team, even knowing they have no idea who I really am. A story of going from homeless to the Ivy League in a decade has given me a certain serenity, and my public transformation was its capstone.

Now I can bring honor to my grandfather's athletic legacy while establishing an academic legacy for my own children. These steps through Franklin Field may repeat daily, but they've signaled the end of a long journey for which I once thought there would never be an end. These bricks will too know my name as well as my footprints, for I have given my children a story worth sharing of their own.

Marissa Alexa McCool

Rhythms of Chaos

To stand at the top of Franklin Field is a simultaneously isolating and all-encompassing experience. The perch atop the 19th-century brick stadium allows ubiquitous visibility of the entire building, but also a landscape view of South Philadelphia from a few hundred feet in the air. For one to filter the sounds requires a tremendous amount of effort, as left unfiltered, the combination of the urban and the athletic makes for absolute chaos.

As I focus toward the downward metal slope of the bleachers, the most obvious of sounds are the coaches' whistles, which can be regimental in their timing for exercise cues, notification of a misstep on the player's part, or a forewarning of the head coach's booming expletive-laced shout. From this height, Coach's yelling can't be made out, but his tone indicates that he isn't pleased with what just happened.

Right behind me is the five-foot brick wall preventing me from a quick drop to the SEPTA Line. Just beyond its protecting layers is the Schuylkill Expressway, stretching out parallel to the train tracks. Practice is during mid-afternoon, so the patrons of Philadelphia's notorious highway are slamming on their brakes and honking their horns in excess. The sounds of stress, frustration, and the desire to get home as soon as possible amplify from the South Philadelphia transit system with urgency.

I focus specifically on the 346A entrance ramp, University of Pennsylvania's access point near Franklin Field, and hear the roaring engines of cars running the arrow no longer pointing left causing the emanating horns from elsewhere. The roadway has only two lanes to and from one of the biggest cities in the country, which is responsible for backups nearly all times of the day. I've spent many days and nights hoping the line of cars would start moving eventually.

All together, the chaos of Philadelphia can easily be summarized into the rhythm of engines with the melody of horns. Diesel engines bring loads across the bypass trestles, adding a deep humming of a firing locomotive to the uneven keel of thousands of automobiles. The train horn, much louder than that of the automotive commuters, pierces through the afternoon sky, alerting any foolish enough to trespass on railroad property that it would be advisable to immediately abandon doing so.

This urban soundtrack speaks to the atmosphere that Center City Philadelphia is known for providing: angry, urgent, impatient people just wanting you to get out of their way. From this height, only the angry are heard, and their call is the horn. Maybe it's for cutting them off, maybe it's because they're just having a bad day, but it's inevitable. The commercialized jungle placates the American spirit of professionalized stress, only encouraging its continued sponsorship from the state.

I'd rather turn back toward the practicing kids, now sounding off with the counting of their push-ups to the coach's satisfaction. Both sights are equally regimented, and in some ways quite similar in their execution. Either side displays rhythms of chaos, which likely isn't too dissimilar from any urban environment.

Ghosts of a Memory

Many concrete plaques cover the red bricks of Franklin Field. Countless names list accomplishments, from track and field records of the Penn Relays, the early football legends that made Penn a powerhouse, and Ben Franklin, for whom the stadium (and everything else on campus) was named. These engravings stare at the current young crop of players fighting for another Ivy League championship with their blood and sweat while I contribute my small part from the booth on the top row.

It makes one humble to stand with the real, original Heisman Trophy, as almost no one remembers that he played and coached here. The banners show seventeen "Ivy League Football Champion" teams, but hidden amongst them are seven national championship winners before the Ivies stopped giving athletic scholarships. That's still tied for seventh all-time, and Penn stopped giving athletic scholarships in 1954.

I wrote in my first essay how I thought of the ghosts that crossed those end zone lines, some of them going back to when the game was first invented. Penn is one of the Ancient 8, an affectionate term given to those eight schools who would become the Ivy League later, but worked out all the kinks of the game itself in order to establish it as the powerhouse entertainment juggernaut it would become.

Now, on a good day, we may get 20,000 for the homecoming game. This stadium once held sixty to seventy thousand fans for both Ivy League and Philadelphia Eagles games alike, and the ghosts of past national success now waver in the presence of the academic prestige Penn retains. Those standards, conversely, weed out those of lesser character and leave only those of great integrity playing for the Penn Quakers.

I've spent so much time with these kids in the last few years that I'm hoping to one day see them playing on national television. Our quarterback for sure will bring back memories of the days when Penn Quakers were number one draft picks without a second glance. There are reasons that three football trophies of accomplishment are named after former Quaker players and coaches.

While I spend a great deal of time with these kids, I can't help but think of who I once was, who I am now, and who I present. I give a lot for these kids, but among those things is not my true identity. They see my past, who I once pretended to be, and how my slowly-changing body still presents to those not in the know. Internally though, change has never been more drastic. The meds do their job, my body starts to correct itself, but I know that even among jocks of high character, remaining closeted is for the benefit. I was tormented for far too long by their type to risk it now with so little time remaining for me here at Penn, but once I move on to grad school, what they saw will only be a ghost of a memory.

Coming Out

This is the day.

This is the day I chose to be myself, in public, in the daylight, at university for the very first time. What safer day than Halloween, right?

The stares from passers-by were still quite obvious, and I heard the comments likely not meant for my ears.

"I forgot that it's Halloween."

"I think that's a guy."

"What's with the makeup?"

Those are things I've heard every time I've dressed like this. Even among this class of friends, it's tempting to initially call it a costume, but it isn't. What they see every other day is a costume, one that I've grown tired of wearing but don't feel safe enough to take off.

Except for today. Today is the day that a 6'3" person like myself can walk down Locust Walk and not have to worry as much. Ironically, it's the exact same spot where I was the only time I missed class, and I screamed my identity at a hate-preacher. How quickly I've progressed.

I've been on hormones for over three months. It's the best decision I've ever made, and one day I will look like this every single day. But the stares won't change. The comments won't change. Even at such a supposedly-liberal school, it's inevitable. I shouldn't have to fear for my own safety for expressing myself, but trans people are murdered in this city. Bills are passed to deny us the right to be people, and I'm not supposed to be scared.

My classmates mean well, and I'm grateful for how nice they all were to me, especially when they found out this wasn't a costume. But it's hard to articulate just how terrifying it can be to look like this any other day of the year. It's hard to describe what it's like to be suspicious of every person, wondering if they watch FOX News or go to the Hate Preacher's church and are just waiting for a chance to make an example of an unsuspecting trans person.

I'm really tall. I pretend to be masculine enough so that the football team won't be suspicious. But thirty-one years of wearing this mask except around close friends has been too much, and I know this reality is inevitable. This time, however, I'm doing it at my own pace, and today took a lot of self-convincing. I changed my mind several times this morning alone, but still went through with it. If not now, when? Right?

If anything motivated me, it's the election of a man who fully intends to regress all rights we've gained over the past eight years. He was elected to remind us that we weren't as human as we thought we were. He's made the country a gendered space again, or at least a binary-gendered space. Doesn't make it okay either way.

My name is Ris. Everyone here knows me as Alex. That's okay, for now. I know at least here I'll be safe.

Instagram: The Town

Rows of autumn leaves reach out from their extended branches along the golden-lit highway. These weren't visible last night, when a truck overturning on I-95 led to a two hour delay. The town from which I was leaving remained fresh in my memory as a moment suspended in time, much like the little town itself.

I feel so condescendingly quaint, describing Portland, Maine as a little town, but as I reminded the friend I met there, I go to school in Philadelphia. The red brick sidewalks guiding your stroll to the best brunch I've ever had, the trees shaking hands with the architecture of varying ages, people who aren't complete assholes... I wasn't sure how to handle it at this point in my life.

To cross the New Hampshire border is a visual delight; the steel beams impede viewing the images of old industry, new gentrification, and shimmering water. A fall day in Maine leaves me with hours left to travel, but a million thoughts to sort as well. I'd just spent an entire day as myself, dressed as myself, acting like myself, and acknowledging myself, and I couldn't have done it in a safer place. Even the head shop had a pride flag out front, and surprisingly enough, Hell itself didn't unleash and point a finger at the weird tranny in purple bondage pants. It's pleasant what can happen when people aren't shitbags to total strangers in public, yet this town's level of not giving a single fuck surprise even me.

If Instagram was a town, it'd be Portland. Everyone dresses like what the rest of America thinks is a hipster, but instead of being patronizing, they say hi and compliment you on your manicure. They offer freshly-squeezed orange juice and gently touch your back after excusing themselves. I couldn't Photoshop a more concise image of what the American electorate thinks is wrong with America, so why exactly was I so comfortable there? What is it about people like me and the fine brunch crowd of Portland, Maine that is such a threat... I mean, beyond of course using the appropriate restroom, which I did, and amazingly no one was sexually assaulted. After all, the president-elect wasn't there, so it was a safer bet that way.

The drive through New Hampshire is so short that you could miss it if you sneezed. I leave as quickly as Quaker athletes bolt after a game with the Big Green. The season is over, so I no longer have to make extra efforts to hide my identity three days a week. With a safe class and the most amazing, supportive reaction I could've hoped for, my sudden burst of assertiveness and confidence only shines brighter as my head bobs to the beat of the tunes playing.

No longer giving any semblance of a shit for the time being, I still have four states to go. The fall light and autumn's bright won't last much longer, but my smile will reflect the kindness of Portland for days to come.

Escaping the Danger of Reality as a Girl

I waved people off, pretending that I was okay to avoid attention. I clutched my inner regions, feeling them reject something. My vision blurry and my mind racing, I got in the passenger side of the car and hoped he wasn't following me.

Having not been socialized as a girl most of my life, I was a prime target for manipulators. I never had to learn many of the tragic lessons so many of us do from a young age. The kinship I felt with most women, even at a very young age, was a strong indicator of whom I was to later truly become.

The last few months had been so life-affirming. There I was, living out in the open, finding out how much more comfortable I was while presenting female. That night, I'd used the women's bathroom, and amazingly, nobody was assaulted in the process. Critics use us as reasons to boycott Target, because they acknowledge us as people, but I remember how it was to be on the inside of a girls' moment. The emptiness that had consumed me for years made sense.

Guys were talking to me, and one of them offered me a drink. That was something that when pretending to be a man, I never even had to consider. When I sipped on the drink, I doubled over and nearly collapsed. Wow, nothing had ever hit me like that before! But maybe it was just something that I'd never tried and I wasn't expecting it, right?

My friend Natalie stayed with me, and the way she spoke to me as a fellow girl intoxicated me. This was right. How long had I been lying to everyone else, but most of all, myself?

But the man with the drink wouldn't stop touching me. Even after I said no. Nat did her best to protect me. At one point, she lifted her leg over the front of my dress to block his advances, saying, "she is a lady. Start treating her like one." It didn't make him stop though. Nothing did. He kept saying, "we don't even have to have sex." As if that was some kind of safety assurance, since sex is of course expected as a trans woman.

Once more, he offered me a drink, and that's when reality hit me like a Neo-Nazi at a pride rally; it was the same cup. Same amount of liquid still in it, my lipstick still on the edge of the plastic. It wasn't my inability to handle alcohol, I'd been roofied. All I wanted was an escape. My body was no longer mine, and had I drank the whole thing, I might've lost complete control.

I sighed as the lights from the club disappeared into a fading darkness. I had to escape this danger by de-transitioning my own mind. The car driving away helped me escape that night, but I had to fall back into hiding to escape the pain of the danger of being myself.

Walking in Baltimore, Then and Now

Every step I took down the cold concrete streets of Baltimore could've been my last, and I didn't even realize I needed to worry about that until years later.

As I now duck my head and try not to make eye contact on Locust Walk, I remember beaming with my near-seven-foot frame in stiletto heels. The boots were a few sizes too small, which just pushed me up higher, but I didn't care. On this walk, I didn't consider myself transgender, mostly because I didn't know that was a thing. At that point, I thought it was being a drag queen.

I allow my hair to drift in my face, avoiding full eye contact with the group of guys walking in the other direction. Why do I have to feel these two extremes so close to each other? I leave English as confident as I've ever been in who I am and how I look, and by the time I get to Critical Writing, I'm a nervous wreck hoping not to be jumped.

I could've been jumped in Baltimore. Baltimore's not as big of a city as Philadelphia, but it has a reputation. With so many Otaku in town for the convention, how would they have noticed some tall kid getting quietly mugged? Besides, "he" was in heels anyway, he should've known better, right?

My leather boots caress the soft red bricks, prepared to strike out if anyone gets any ideas. Apparently the apologists think that not wanting to live this way was a boutique issue and that's why we deserve blame for Trump. How often do they have to walk on their own campus on high-alert at literally all times?

I passed that night in the convention. Nobody gave me any trouble, and most didn't know it was a "guy" until I spoke. I hadn't yet started using the feminine voice, but I didn't know I was allowed to either. All the sex education we got, and no one ever mentioned anything about gender transition.

Creeps could've been lurking behind me that night. Now it's harder to tell who might be a threat. They don't all wear white hoods and Confederate flags. I accept that I stand out, but also that I'd rather stand out for who I am than lie to myself. If my campus can't be a safe place, I'll be ready for when it's not.

Perhaps all I've lost from that night in Baltimore is the slim figure, but there's a part of me that would love to have that oblivion, that lack of worry that something might happen to me.

But eigteen-year-old me wasn't being honest with herself, and thirty-one-year-old me is, and with knowledge comes doubt. With the election, I need to be on alert, so that if the creeps go after me, I'm ready to kick their throat with my flat boots. I'm not as tall as I was that night in Baltimore, but I stand taller now than I ever have.

Once Unspoken

A Monologue

To the world, I'm thirty-one. To myself, I'm thirteen.
13 years ago, that's when I got my name.
The name that would stick in my mind,
The name I would crave to be called,
The name that made me cry at night,
The name that made me wish it'd gone away,
That was the name that stayed in my heart.

A drag queen is what I thought I was,
Because I didn't know any better.
We weren't educated on such things.
Even the open-minded among us,
To our groups, conversations, and movies,
Trans people existed only as
Jokes
Punch-Lines
Comedy

Fodder
Plot Twists.
That was all we knew.

Drag queen is what I let them call me,
To pretend that I was laughing with them,
Instead of believing the laughter was at me.
But I loved the makeup, the clothes, the shoes,
The way my eyes looked with mascara,
The way my legs felt smooth to the touch,
The way I felt unapologetically myself,
And nobody could take that from me.

But I had to keep it a secret.
It was too much for some people to handle.
They thought I should be a real man,
Be a provider, protector, breadwinner,
The cuddler, the kisser, the initiator,
Even those who said they understood,
Appreciated the dynamic,
Thought it was kinda hot,
Always defaulted to the traditional expectation.
Too emotional, too needy, too affectionate,
"Stop trying to be the little spoon!"
"Stop being scared at loud noises!"
"Stop wearing such bright colors!"
"Stop skipping, stop dancing, stop singing,
Stop wearing eyeliner, stop tilting your head,
Stop putting your hand on your hip,
Stop being so…
Girly!"

Growing up pretending to be a boy,
Girly was the worst thing you could be.
You play like a girl, you cry like a girl,
You were a pussy if you were weak,
You were a girlfriend if you didn't like guns,
Girls couldn't rape guys because,
Huh-huh, you can't rape the willing, LOL, right?
Hey baby, you don't need the gun!
High-five, bro!

I craved to be protected.
I adored feeling like people wanted
To stand up for me
To let me cry
To let them be there for me,
But I couldn't.
I wasn't being honest with myself
Because I was scared.
Terrified.
What would the world think?
What would my parents think?
What would happen to me?
Would I be bullied?
Beaten?
Assaulted?
Killed?

Then I found the Queer Dictionary.
I read through the words, the labels, the definitions.
I wasn't a drag queen.
I wasn't a crossdresser.
Transgender though, that seemed right.

But it was too much commitment.
So I went with gender queer,
Non-binary,
Genderfluid,
Gender nonconforming...
Anything that allowed me to be Marissa,
But not take the full jump.
No hormones, no shots, no meds,
Nothing permanent.
Permanent was scary.

However, as I became Marissa,
I stopped liking being called sir.
I began to hate my deadname.
I began to hate being associated as a guy,
A male,
A him,
A dude,
A bro,
Thank you very much, sir.
Have a nice day, sir.
Is this your husband?
Is this your father?

I wanted to be one of the girls.
I wanted to be a girl.
I... am a girl.
I couldn't even commit to it when I went on HRT,
But my spouse referred to me as Marissa,
Ris,
Rissy Monster,
Princess,

Baby.
He called me beautiful, precious,
Pretty, princess, baby girl…
All the things I wanted to be called my entire life,
But wasn't allowed.
Cause that'd be gay, right?

But then…
Then two people took from me.
Like thieves in the night, they stole.
They took my body.
They took my rights.
They took my voice.
They took
My consent.
I hid.
I ran.
I fled.
I became numb.
Distant.
Vacant.
I cut my hair.
Ditched outfits.
Tossed aside the makeup.
Died inside every time someone called me Alex,
But I dealt with it.
Because that's what the world was like
To people like me
If I was true.

Then one day, he came to our school.
Pastor Carl.

Filled with hate,
Bigotry,
Moral superiority,
Slurs,
Threats,
Damnation,
Scare-tactics,
Humiliation,
And self-righteousness.
He called girls sluts,
Gay people words I won't repeat,
And trans acceptance was the reason
Penn had a suicide problem.
Not because of bullies like him,
But because being who we are
Was subconscious defiance of truth.
That's why we hurt,
That's why we suffered,
That's why we died,
Because Pastor Carl knew the truth
And we ran from it.
We only chose to be who we were
To mock God.

As I stood up to him,
I was no longer afraid.
Nothing he said could touch me.
Nothing he said could penetrate my shield.
Nothing he said mattered.
So I yelled directly in his face:
"I'm transgender, fuck you!"
And that was it.

I was out.
I was Marissa.

Then we got a new president,
And all hell broke loose.
The same fear I'd had for years,
Seemed to consume the many.
So I wrote,
Yelled,
Podcasted,
Published,
Guested,
Stood up,
Stood out,
Owned who I was,
And within three months,
I was Marissa fuckin' McCool.
Published author,
LGBT columnist,
Trans-podcaster,
Guest on God Awful Movies,
And now, performing in the Vagina Monologues.
As me.
As Marissa.
As Marissa Alexa McCool.
Who I've always been.
True.

Tonight is not my first, or even hundredth
Time on stage in public,
But it is the first time,
The very first time,

That any cast list or program
Will read: Marissa Alexa McCool.
And that, my dear friends,
Was worth every step of the journey.